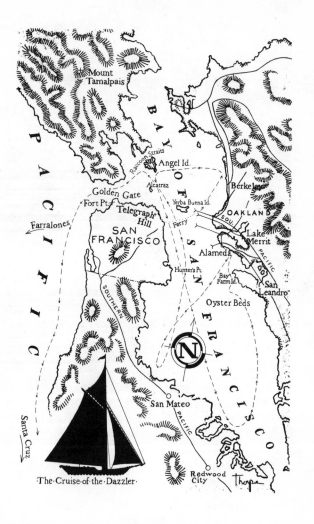

The·Cruise·of·the·Dazzler·

THE CRUISE OF THE
DAZZLER

JACK LONDON

Illustrations by Peter Thorpe

Star Rover House
Oakland, California
MCMLXXXI

Copyright © 1981
by
Star Rover House

Library of Congress Catalog Number
ISBN 0-932458-06-8

Hardbound 200 copies.
Softbound 1000 copies.
526

Star Rover House
306-12th Street
Oakland, California 94607

CONTENTS

Contents

LIST OF ILLUSTRATIONS

PAGE

THE CRUISE OF THE DAZZLER

CHAPTER I

BROTHER AND SISTER

THEY ran across the shining sand, the Pacific thundering its long surge at their backs, and when they gained the roadway leaped upon bicycles and dived at faster pace into the green avenues of the park. There were three of them, three boys, in as many bright-colored sweaters, and they " scorched " along the cycle-path as dangerously near the speed-limit as is the custom of boys in bright-colored sweaters to go. They may have exceeded the speed-limit. A mounted park policeman thought so, but was not

3

sure, and contented himself with cautioning them as they flashed by. They acknowledged the warning promptly, and on the next turn of the path as promptly forgot it, which is also a custom of boys in bright-colored sweaters.

Shooting out through the entrance to Golden Gate Park, they turned into San Francisco, and took the long sweep of the descending hills at a rate that caused pedestrians to turn and watch them anxiously. Through the city streets the bright sweaters flew, turning and twisting to escape climbing the steeper hills, and, when the steep hills were unavoidable, doing stunts to see which would first gain the top.

The boy who more often hit up the pace, led the scorching, and instituted the stunts was called Joe by his companions. It was "follow the leader," and he led, the merriest and boldest in the bunch. But as they pedaled into the Western Addition, among the large and comfortable residences, his laughter became less loud and frequent, and he unconsciously lagged in the rear. At Laguna and Vallejo streets his companions turned off to the right.

"So long, Fred," he called as he turned his wheel to the left. "So long, Charley."

"See you to-night!" they called back.

"No — I can't come," he answered.

"Aw, come on," they begged.

"No, I 've got to dig. — So long!"

As he went on alone, his face grew grave and a vague worry came into his eyes. He began resolutely to whistle, but this dwindled away till it was a thin and very subdued little sound, which ceased altogether as he rode up the driveway to a large two-storied house.

"Oh, Joe!"

He hesitated before the door to the library. Bessie was there, he knew, studiously working up her lessons. She must be nearly through with them, too, for she was always done before dinner, and dinner could not be many minutes away. As for his lessons, they were as yet untouched. The thought made him angry. It was bad enough to have one's sister— and two years younger at that— in the same grade, but to have her continually head and shoulders above him in scholarship was a most intolerable thing. Not that he was dull. No one knew better than himself that he was not dull. But somehow— he did not quite know how — his mind was on other things and he was usually unprepared.

"Joe — please come here." There was the slightest possible plaintive note in her voice this time.

"Well?" he said, thrusting aside the portière with an impetuous movement.

He said it gruffly, but he was half sorry for it the next instant when he saw a slender little girl regarding him with wistful eyes across the big reading-table heaped with books. She was curled up, with pencil and pad, in an easy-chair of such generous dimensions that it made her seem more delicate and fragile than she really was.

"What is it, Sis?" he asked more gently, crossing over to her side.

She took his hand in hers and pressed it against her cheek, and as he stood beside her came closer to him with a nestling movement.

"What is the matter, Joe dear?" she asked softly. "Won't you tell me?"

He remained silent. It struck him as ridiculous to confess his troubles to a little sister, even if her reports *were* higher than his. And the little sister struck him as ridiculous to demand his troubles of him. "What a soft cheek she has!" he thought as she pressed her face gently against his hand. If he could but tear himself away — it was all so foolish! Only he might hurt her feelings, and, in his experience, girls' feelings were very easily hurt.

She opened his fingers and kissed the palm of his hand. It was like a rose-leaf falling; it was also her way of asking her question over again.

"Nothing's the matter," he said decisively. And then, quite inconsistently, he blurted out, "Father!"

His worry was now in her eyes. "But father is so good and kind, Joe," she began. "Why don't you try to please him? He does n't ask much of you, and it's all for your own good. It's not as though you were a fool, like some boys. If you would only study a little bit—"

"That's it! Lecturing!" he exploded, tearing his hand roughly away. "Even you are beginning to lecture me now. I suppose the cook and the stable-boy will be at it next."

He shoved his hands into his pockets and looked forward into a melancholy and desolate future filled with interminable lectures and lecturers innumerable.

"Was that what you wanted me for?" he demanded, turning to go.

She caught at his hand again. "No, it was n't; only you looked so worried that I thought—I—" Her voice broke, and she began again freshly. "What I wanted to tell you was that we 're planning a trip across the bay to Oakland, next Saturday, for a tramp in the hills."

"Who 's going?"

"Myrtle Hayes—"

"What! That little softy?" he interrupted.

"I don't think she is a softy," Bessie answered with spirit. "She 's one of the sweetest girls I know."

"Which is n't saying much, considering the girls you know. But go on. Who are the others?"

"Pearl Sayther, and her sister Alice, and Jessie Hilborn, and Sadie French, and Edna Crothers. That 's all the girls."

Joe sniffed disdainfully. "Who are the fellows, then?"

"Maurice and Felix Clement, Dick Schofield, Burt Layton, and—"

9

"That's enough. Milk-and-water chaps, all of them."

"I—I wanted to ask you and Fred and Charley," she said in a quavering voice. "That's what I called you in for—to ask you to come."

"And what are you going to do?" he asked.

"Walk, gather wild flowers,—the poppies are all out now,—eat luncheon at some nice place, and—and—"

"Come home," he finished for her.

Bessie nodded her head. Joe put his hands in his pockets again, and walked up and down.

"A sissy outfit, that's what it is," he said abruptly; "and a sissy program. None of it in mine, please."

She tightened her trembling lips and struggled on bravely. "What would you rather do?" she asked.

"I'd sooner take Fred and Charley and go off somewhere and do something — well, anything."

He paused and looked at her. She was waiting patiently for him to proceed. He was aware of his inability to express in words what he felt and wanted, and all his trouble and general dissatisfaction rose up and gripped hold of him.

"Oh, you can't understand!" he burst out. "You can't understand. You 're a girl. You like to be prim and neat, and to be good in deportment and ahead in your studies. You don't care for danger and adventure and such things, and you don't care for boys who are rough, and have life and go in them, and all that. You like good little boys in white collars, with clothes always clean and hair always combed, who like to stay in at recess and be petted by the teacher and told how they 're always up in their studies; nice little boys who never get into scrapes— who are too busy walking around and picking flowers and eating lunches with girls, to get into scrapes. Oh, I know the kind—afraid of their own shadows,

11

and no more spunk in them than in so
many sheep. That 's what they are—
sheep. Well, I 'm not a sheep, and
there 's no more to be said. And I don't
want to go on your picnic, and, what 's
more, I 'm not going."

The tears welled up in Bessie's brown
eyes, and her lips were trembling. This
angered him unreasonably. What were
girls good for, anyway?— always blub-
bering, and interfering, and carrying on.
There was no sense in them.

"A fellow can't say anything without
making you cry," he began, trying to
appease her. "Why, I did n't mean anything, Sis. I did n't, sure. I—"

He paused helplessly and looked down
at her. She was sobbing, and at the
same time shaking with the effort to control her sobs, while big tears were rolling
down her cheeks.

"Oh, you — you girls!" he cried, and
strode wrathfully out of the room.

CHAPTER II

"THE DRACONIAN REFORMS"

A FEW minutes later, and still wrath-ful, Joe went in to dinner. He ate silently, though his father and mother and Bessie kept up a genial flow of con-versation. There she was, he communed savagely with his plate, crying one minute, and the next all smiles and laughter. Now that was n't his way. If *he* had anything sufficiently important to cry about, rest assured he would n't get over it for days. Girls were hypocrites, that was all there was to it. They did n't feel one hundredth part of all that they said when they cried. It stood to reason that they did n't. It must be that they just carried on because they enjoyed it. It made them feel good to make other people miserable, especially boys. That was why they were always interfering.

Thus reflecting sagely, he kept his eyes on his plate and did justice to the fare; for one cannot scorch from the Cliff House to the Western Addition via the park without being guilty of a healthy appetite.

Now and then his father directed a glance at him in a certain mildly anxious way. Joe did not see these glances, but Bessie saw them, every one. Mr. Bronson was a middle-aged man, well developed and of heavy build, though not fat. His was a rugged face, square-jawed and stern-featured, though his eyes were kindly and there were lines about the mouth that betokened laughter rather than severity. A close examination was not required to discover the resemblance between him and Joe. The same broad forehead and strong jaw characterized them both, and the eyes, taking into consideration the difference of age, were as like as peas from one pod.

"How are you getting on, Joe?" Mr. Bronson asked finally. Dinner was over and they were about to leave the table.

"Oh, I don't know," Joe answered carelessly, and then added: "We have examinations to-morrow. I'll know then."

"Whither bound?" his mother questioned, as he turned to leave the room. She was a slender, willowy woman, whose brown eyes Bessie's were, and likewise her tender ways.

"To my room," Joe answered. "To work," he supplemented.

She rumpled his hair affectionately, and bent and kissed him. Mr. Bronson smiled approval at him as he went out, and he hurried up the stairs, resolved to dig hard and pass the examinations of the coming day.

Entering his room, he locked the door and sat down at a desk most comfortably arranged for a boy's study. He ran his eye over his text-books. The history examination came the first thing in the morning, so he would begin on that. He opened the book where a page was turned down, and began to read:

Shortly after the Draconian reforms, a war broke out between Athens and Megara respecting the island of Salamis, to which both cities laid claim.

That was easy; but what were the Draconian reforms? He must look them up. He felt quite studious as he ran over the back pages, till he chanced to raise his eyes above the top of the book and saw on a chair a baseball mask and a catcher's glove. They should n't have lost that game last Saturday, he thought, and they would n't have, either, if it had n't been for Fred. He wished Fred would n't fumble so. He could hold a hundred difficult balls in succession, but when a critical point came, he 'd let go of even a dewdrop. He 'd have to send him out in

the field and bring in Jones to first base.
Only Jones was so excitable. He could
hold any kind of a ball, no matter how
critical the play was, but there was no
telling what he would do with the ball
after he got it.

Joe came to himself with a start. A
pretty way of studying history! He
buried his head in his book and began:

Shortly after the Draconian reforms—

He read the sentence through three
times, and then recollected that he had
not looked up the Draconian reforms.

A knock came at the door. He turned
the pages over with a noisy flutter, but
made no answer.

The knock was repeated, and Bessie's
" Joe, dear " came to his ears.

" What do you want? " he demanded.
But before she could answer he hurried
on: " No admittance. I 'm busy."

" I came to see if I could help you,"

she pleaded. "I 'm all done, and I thought —"

"Of course you 're all done!" he shouted. "You always are!"

He held his head in both his hands to keep his eyes on the book. But the baseball mask bothered him. The more he attempted to keep his mind on the history the more in his mind's eye he saw the mask resting on the chair and all the games in which it had played its part.

This would never do. He deliberately placed the book face downward on the desk and walked over to the chair. With a swift sweep he sent both mask and glove hurtling under the bed, and so violently that he heard the mask rebound from the wall.

Shortly after the Draconian reforms, a war broke out between Athens and Megara —

The mask had rolled back from the wall. He wondered if it had rolled back far enough for him to see it. No, he would n't look. What did it matter if it had rolled out? That was n't history. He wondered —

He peered over the top of the book, and there was the mask peeping out at him from under the edge of the bed. This was not to be borne. There was no use attempting to study while that mask was around. He went over and fished it out, crossed the room to the closet, and tossed it inside, then locked the door. That was settled, thank goodness! Now he could do some work.

He sat down again.

Shortly after the Draconian reforms, a war broke out between Athens and Megara respecting the island of Salamis, to which both cities laid claim.

Which was all very well, if he had only found out what the Draconian reforms were. A soft glow pervaded the room, and he suddenly became aware of it. What could cause it? He looked out of the window. The setting sun was slanting its long rays against low-hanging masses of summer clouds, turning them to warm scarlet and rosy red; and it was from them that the red light, mellow and glowing, was flung earthward.

His gaze dropped from the clouds to the bay beneath. The sea-breeze was dying down with the day, and off Fort Point a fishing-boat was creeping into port before the last light breeze. A little beyond, a tug was sending up a twisted pillar of smoke as it towed a three-masted schooner to sea. His eyes wandered over toward the Marin County shore. The line where land and water met was already in darkness, and long shadows were creeping up the hills toward Mount Tamalpais, which was sharply silhouetted against the western sky.

Oh, if he, Joe Bronson, were only on that fishing-boat and sailing in with a deep-sea catch! Or if he were on that

schooner, heading out into the sunset, into
the world! That was life, that was living, doing something and being something in the world. And, instead, here he
was, pent up in a close room, racking his
brains about people dead and gone thou-
sands of years before he was born.

He jerked himself away from the
window as though held there by some
physical force, and resolutely carried his
chair and history into the farthest corner
of the room, where he sat down with his
back to the window.

An instant later, so it seemed to him,
he found himself again staring out of the
window and dreaming. How he had got
there he did not know. His last recollection was the finding of a subheading on
a page on the right-hand side of the book
which read: " The Laws and Constitu-
tion of Draco." And then, evidently like
walking in one's sleep, he had come to
the window. How long had he been
there? he wondered. The fishing-boat

which he had seen off Fort Point was now crawling into Meiggs's Wharf. This denoted nearly an hour's lapse of time. The sun had long since set; a solemn grayness was brooding over the water, and the first faint stars were beginning to twinkle over the crest of Mount Tamalpais.

He turned, with a sigh, to go back into his corner, when a long whistle, shrill and piercing, came to his ears. That was Fred. He sighed again. The whistle repeated itself. Then another whistle joined it. That was Charley. They were waiting on the corner — lucky fellows!

Well, they would n't see him this night. Both whistles arose in duet. He writhed in his chair and groaned. No, they would n't see him this night, he reiterated, at the same time rising to his feet. It was certainly impossible for him to join them when he had not yet learned about the Draconian reforms. The same force which had held him to the window now seemed drawing him across the room to the desk. It made him put the history on top of his school-books, and he had the door unlocked and was half-way into the hall before he realized it. He started to return, but the thought came to him that he could go out for a little while and then come back and do his work.

A very little while, he promised himself, as he went down-stairs. He went down faster and faster, till at the bottom he was going three steps at a time. He popped his cap on his head and went out of the side entrance in a rush ; and ere he reached the corner the reforms of Draco were as far away in the past as Draco himself, while the examinations on the morrow were equally far away in the future.

CHAPTER III

"WHAT 'S up?" Joe asked, as he joined Fred and Charley.

"Kites," Charley answered. "Come on. We 're tired out waiting for you."

The three set off down the street to the brow of the hill, where they looked down upon Union Street, far below and almost under their feet. This they called the Pit, and it was well named. Themselves they called the Hill-dwellers, and a descent into the Pit by the Hill-dwellers was looked upon by them as a great adventure.

Scientific kite-flying was one of the keenest pleasures of these three particular Hill-dwellers, and six or eight kites

24

strung out on a mile of twine and soaring into the clouds was an ordinary achievement for them. They were compelled to replenish their kite-supply often ; for whenever an accident occurred, and the string broke, or a ducking kite dragged down the rest, or the wind suddenly died out, their kites fell into the Pit, from which place they were unrecoverable. The reason for this was the young people of the Pit were a piratical and robber race with peculiar ideas of ownership and property rights.

On a day following an accident to a kite of one of the Hill-dwellers, the self-same kite could be seen riding the air attached to a string which led down into the Pit to the lairs of the Pit People. So it came about that the Pit People, who were a poor folk and unable to afford scientific kite-flying, developed great proficiency in the art when their neighbors the Hill-dwellers took it up.

There was also an old sailorman who

profited by this recreation of the Hill-dwellers ; for he was learned in sails and air-currents, and being deft of hand and cunning, he fashioned the best-flying kites that could be obtained. He lived in a rattletrap shanty close to the water, where he could still watch with dim eyes the ebb and flow of the tide, and the ships pass out and in, and where he could revive old memories of the days when he, too, went down to the sea in ships.

To reach his shanty from the Hill one had to pass through the Pit, and thither the three boys were bound. They had often gone for kites in the daytime, but this was their first trip after dark, and they felt it to be, as it indeed was, a hazardous adventure.

In simple words, the Pit was merely the cramped and narrow quarters of the poor, where many nationalities crowded together in cosmopolitan confusion, and lived as best they could, amid much dirt and squalor. It was still early evening

when the boys passed through on their
way to the sailorman's shanty, and no mishap befell them, though some of the Pit
boys stared at them savagely and hurled
a taunting remark after them, now and
then.

The sailorman made kites which were
not only splendid fliers but which folded
up and were very convenient to carry.
Each of the boys bought a few, and,
with them wrapped in compact bundles
and under their arms, started back on the
return journey.

"Keep a sharp lookout for the b'ys,"
the kite-maker cautioned them. "They 're
like to be cruisin' round after dark."

"We 're not afraid," Charley assured
him; "and we know how to take care
of ourselves."

Used to the broad and quiet streets of
the Hill, the boys were shocked and
stunned by the life that teemed in the
close-packed quarter. It seemed some
thick and monstrous growth of vegeta-

tion, and that they were wading through
it. They shrank closely together in the
tangle of narrow streets as though for
protection, conscious of the strangeness
of it all, and how unrelated they were
to it.

Children and babies sprawled on the
sidewalk and under their feet. Bare-
headed and unkempt women gossiped in
the doorways or passed back and forth with
scant marketings in their arms. There
was a general odor of decaying fruit and
fish, a smell of staleness and putridity.
Big hulking men slouched by, and ragged
little girls walked gingerly through the
confusion with foaming buckets of beer
in their hands. There was a clatter and
garble of foreign tongues and brogues,
shrill cries, quarrels and wrangles, and the
Pit pulsed with a great and steady mur-
mur, like the hum of the human hive that
it was.

"Phew! I'll be glad when we're out
of it," Fred said.

He spoke in a whisper, and Joe and Charley nodded grimly that they agreed with him. They were not inclined to speech, and they walked as rapidly as the crowd permitted, with much the same feelings as those of travelers in a dangerous and hostile jungle.

And danger and hostility stalked in the Pit. The inhabitants seemed to resent the presence of these strangers from the Hill. Dirty little urchins abused them as they passed, snarling with assumed bravery, and prepared to run away at the first sign of attack. And still other little urchins formed a noisy parade at the heels of the boys, and grew bolder with increasing numbers.

"Don't mind them," Joe cautioned. "Take no notice, but keep right on. We'll soon be out of it."

"No; we're in for it," said Fred, in an undertone. "Look there!"

On the corner they were approaching, four or five boys of about their own age were standing. The light from a street-lamp fell upon them and disclosed one with vivid red hair. It could be no other than "Brick" Simpson, the redoubtable leader of a redoubtable gang. Twice within their memory he had led his gang up the Hill and spread panic and terror among the Hill-dwelling young folk, who fled wildly to their homes, while their fathers and mothers hurriedly telephoned for the police.

At sight of the group on the corner, the rabble at the heels of the three boys melted away on the instant with like manifestations of fear. This but increased the anxiety of the boys, though they held boldly on their way.

The red-haired boy detached himself from the group, and stepped before them, blocking their path. They essayed to go around him, but he stretched out his arm.

"Wot yer doin' here?" he snarled. "Why don't yer stay where yer b'long?"

"We 're just going home," Fred said mildly.

Brick looked at Joe. "Wot yer got under yer arm?" he demanded.

Joe contained himself and took no heed of him. "Come on," he said to Fred and Charley, at the same time starting to brush past the gang-leader.

But with a quick blow Brick Simpson struck him in the face, and with equal quickness snatched the bundle of kites from under his arm.

Joe uttered an inarticulate cry of rage, and, all caution flung to the winds, sprang at his assailant.

This was evidently a surprise to the gang-leader, who expected least of all to be attacked in his own territory. He retreated backward, still clutching the kites, and divided between desire to fight and desire to retain his capture.

The latter desire dominated him, and he turned and fled swiftly down the narrow side-street into a labyrinth of streets and alleys. Joe knew that he was plunging into the wilderness of the enemy's country, but his sense of both property and pride had been offended, and he took up the pursuit hot-footed.

Fred and Charley followed after, though he outdistanced them, and behind came the three other members of the gang, emitting a whistling call while they ran which was evidently intended for the assembling of the rest of the band. As the chase proceeded, these whistles were answered from many different directions, and soon a score of dark figures were tagging at the heels of Fred and Charley, who, in turn, were straining every muscle to keep the swifter-footed Joe in sight.

Brick Simpson darted into a vacant lot, aiming for a "slip," as such things are called which are prearranged passages through fences and over sheds and houses and around dark holes and corners, where the unfamiliar pursuer must go more care-

Joe pursued Brick

fully and where the chances are many
that he will soon lose the track.

But Joe caught Brick before he could
attain his end, and together they rolled
over and over in the dirt, locked in each
other's arms. By the time Fred and
Charley and the gang had come up, they
were on their feet, facing each other.

"Wot d' ye want, eh?" the red-headed
gang-leader was saying in a bullying
tone. "Wot d' ye want? That 's wot I
wanter know."

"I want my kites," Joe answered.

Brick Simpson's eyes sparkled at the
intelligence. Kites were something he
stood in need of himself.

"Then you 've got to fight fer 'em,"
he announced.

"Why should I fight for them?" Joe
demanded indignantly. "They 're mine."
Which went to show how ignorant he was
of the ideas of ownership and property
rights which obtained among the People
of the Pit.

A chorus of jeers and catcalls went up from the gang, which clustered behind its leader like a pack of wolves.

"Why should I fight for them?" Joe reiterated.

"'Cos I say so," Simpson replied. "An' wot I say goes. Understand?"

But Joe did not understand. He refused to understand that Brick Simpson's word was law in San Francisco, or any part of San Francisco. His love of honesty and right dealing was offended, and all his fighting blood was up.

"You give those kites to me, right here and now," he threatened, reaching out his hand for them.

But Simpson jerked them away. "D' ye know who I am?" he demanded. "I 'm Brick Simpson, an' I don't 'low no one to talk to me in that tone of voice."

"Better leave him alone," Charley whispered in Joe's ear. "What are a few kites? Leave him alone and let's get out of this."

"They 're my kites," Joe said slowly in a dogged manner. "They 're my kites, and I 'm going to have them."

"You can't fight the crowd," Fred interfered; "and if you do get the best of him they 'll all pile on you."

The gang, observing this whispered colloquy, and mistaking it for hesitancy on the part of Joe, set up its wolf-like howling again.

"Afraid! afraid!" the young roughs jeered and taunted. "He 's too high-toned, he is! Mebbe he 'll spoil his nice clean shirt, and then what 'll mama say?"

"Shut up!" their leader snapped authoritatively, and the noise obediently died away.

"Will you give me those kites?" Joe demanded, advancing determinedly.

"Will you fight for 'em?" was Simpson's counter-demand.

"Yes," Joe answered.

"Fight! fight!" the gang began to howl again.

35

"And it's me that'll see fair play," said a man's heavy voice.

All eyes were instantly turned upon the man who had approached unseen and made this announcement. By the electric light, shining brightly on them from the corner, they made him out to be a big, muscular fellow, clad in a working-man's garments. His feet were incased in heavy brogans, a narrow strap of black leather held his overalls about his waist, and a black and greasy cap was on his head. His face was grimed with coal-dust, and a coarse blue shirt, open at the neck, revealed a wide throat and massive chest.

"An' who're you?" Simpson snarled, angry at the interruption.

"None of yer business," the newcomer retorted tartly. "But, if it'll do you any good, I'm a fireman on the China steamers, and, as I said, I'm goin' to see fair play. That's my business. Your business is to give fair play. So pitch in, and don't be all night about it."

The three boys were as pleased by the appearance of the fireman as Simpson and his followers were displeased. They conferred together for several minutes, when Simpson deposited the bundle of kites in the arms of one of his gang and stepped forward.

"Come on, then," he said, at the same time pulling off his coat.

Joe handed his to Fred, and sprang toward Brick. They put up their fists and faced each other. Almost instantly Simpson drove in a fierce blow and ducked cleverly away and out of reach of the blow which Joe returned. Joe felt a sudden respect for the abilities of his antagonist, but the only effect upon him was to arouse all the doggedness of his nature and make him utterly determined to win.

Awed by the presence of the fireman, Simpson's followers confined themselves to cheering Brick and jeering Joe. The two boys circled round and round, attacking, feinting, and guarding, and now one and

37

then the other getting in a telling blow. Their positions were in marked contrast. Joe stood erect, planted solidly on his feet, with legs wide apart and head up. On the other hand, Simpson crouched till his head was nearly lost between his shoulders, and all the while he was in constant motion, leaping and springing and manœuvering in the execution of a score or more of tricks quite new and strange to Joe.

At the end of a quarter of an hour, both were very tired, though Joe was much fresher. Tobacco, ill food, and unhealthy living were telling on the gang-leader, who was panting and sobbing for breath. Though at first (and because of superior skill) he had severely punished Joe, he was now weak and his blows were without force. Growing desperate, he adopted what might be called not an unfair but a mean method of attack: he would manœuver, leap in and strike swiftly, and then, ducking forward, fall to the ground at

Joe's feet. Joe could not strike him while he was down, and so would step back until he could get on his feet again, when the thing would be repeated.

But Joe grew tired of this, and prepared for him. Timing his blow with Simpson's attack, he delivered it just as Simpson was ducking forward to fall. Simpson fell, but he fell over on one side, whither he had been driven by the impact of Joe's fist upon his head. He rolled over and got half-way to his feet, where he remained, crying and gasping. His followers called upon him to get up, and he tried once or twice, but was too exhausted and stunned.

"I give in," he said. "I'm licked."

The gang had become silent and depressed at its leader's defeat.

Joe stepped forward.

"I'll trouble you for those kites," he said to the boy who was holding them.

"Oh, I dunno," said another member of the gang, shoving in between Joe and his property. His hair was also a vivid red. "You 've got to lick me before you kin have 'em."

"I don't see that," Joe said bluntly. "I 've fought and I 've won, and there 's nothing more to it."

"Oh, yes, there is," said the other. "I 'm 'Sorrel-top' Simpson. Brick 's my brother. See?"

And so, in this fashion, Joe learned another custom of the Pit People of which he had been ignorant.

"All right," he said, his fighting blood more fully aroused than ever by the unjustness of the proceeding. "Come on."

Sorrel-top Simpson, a year younger than his brother, proved to be a most unfair fighter, and the good-natured fireman was compelled to interfere several times before the second of the Simpson clan lay on the ground and acknowledged defeat.

This time Joe reached for his kites without the slightest doubt that he was to get them. But still another lad stepped

in between him and his property. The
telltale hair, vividly red, sprouted likewise
on this lad's head, and Joe knew him at
once for what he was, another member of
the Simpson clan. He was a younger edi-
tion of his brothers, somewhat less heavily
built, with a face covered with a vast
quantity of freckles, which showed plainly
under the electric light.

"You don't git them there kites till
you git me," he challenged in a piping
little voice. "I'm 'Reddy' Simpson,
an' you ain't licked the fambly till you've
licked me."

The gang cheered admiringly, and
Reddy stripped a tattered jacket preparatory for the fray.

"Git ready," he said to Joe.

Joe's knuckles were torn, his nose was
bleeding, his lip was cut and swollen, while
his shirt had been ripped down from
throat to waist. Further, he was tired,
and breathing hard.

"How many more are there of you

Simpsons?" he asked. "I've got to get home, and if your family's much larger this thing is liable to keep on all night."

"I'm the last an' the best," Reddy replied. "You gits me an' you gits the kites. Sure."

"All right," Joe sighed. "Come on."

While the youngest of the clan lacked the strength and skill of his elders, he made up for it by a wildcat manner of fighting that taxed Joe severely. Time and again it seemed to him that he must give in to the little whirlwind; but each time he pulled himself together and went doggedly on. For he felt that he was fighting for principle, as his forefathers had fought for principle; also, it seemed to him that the honor of the Hill was at stake, and that he, as its representative, could do nothing less than his very best.

So he held on and managed to endure his opponent's swift and continuous rushes till that young and less experienced person at last wore himself out with his own exertions, and from the ground confessed that, for the first time in its history, the "Simpson fambly was beat."

ALCATRAZ ISLAND

CHAPTER IV

THE BITER BITTEN

BUT life in the Pit at best was a precarious affair, as the three Hill-dwellers were quickly to learn. Before Joe could even possess himself of his kites, his astonished eyes were greeted with the spectacle of all his enemies, the fireman included, taking to their heels in wild flight. As the little girls and urchins had melted away before the Simpson gang, so was melting away the Simpson gang before some new and correspondingly awe-inspiring group of predatory creatures.

Joe heard terrified cries of "Fish gang!" "Fish gang!" from those who fled, and he would have fled himself from

this new danger, only he was breathless
from his last encounter, and knew the im-
possibility of escaping whatever threatened. Fred and Charley felt mighty
longings to run away from a danger
great enough to frighten the redoubtable
Simpson gang and the valorous fireman,
but they could not desert their comrade.

Dark forms broke into the vacant lot,
some surrounding the boys and others
dashing after the fugitives. That the
laggards were overtaken was evidenced
by the cries of distress that went up, and
when later the pursuers returned, they
brought with them the luckless and snarling Brick, still clinging fast to the bundle
of kites.

Joe looked curiously at this latest band
of marauders. They were young men of
from seventeen and eighteen to twenty-
three and -four years of age, and bore the
unmistakable stamp of the hoodlum class.
There were vicious faces among them
— faces so vicious as to make Joe's flesh

creep as he looked at them. A couple grasped him tightly by the arms, and Fred and Charley were similarly held captive.

"Look here, you," said one who spoke with the authority of leader, "we 've got to inquire into this. Wot 's be'n goin' on here? Wot 're you up to, Red-head? Wot you be'n doin'?"

"Ain't be'n doin' nothin'," Simpson whined.

"Looks like it." The leader turned up Brick's face to the electric light. "Who 's been paintin' you up like that?" he demanded.

Brick pointed at Joe, who was forthwith dragged to the front.

"Wot was you scrappin' about?"

"Kites — my kites," Joe spoke up boldly. "That fellow tried to take them away from me. He 's got them under his arm now."

"Oh, he has, has he? Look here, you Brick, we don't put up with stealin' in this territory. See? You never rightly owned nothin'. Come, fork over the kites. Last call."

The leader tightened his grasp threateningly, and Simpson, weeping tears of rage, surrendered the plunder.

"Wot yer got under yer arm?" the leader demanded abruptly of Fred, at the same time jerking out the bundle. "More kites, eh? Reg'lar kite-factory gone and got itself lost," he remarked finally, when he had appropriated Charley's bundle. "Now, wot I wants to know is wot we're goin' to do to you t'ree chaps?" he continued in a judicial tone.

"What for?" Joe demanded hotly. "For being robbed of our kites?"

"Not at all, not at all," the leader responded politely; "but for luggin' kites round these quarters an' causin' all this unseemly disturbance. It's disgraceful; that's wot it is — disgraceful."

At this juncture, when the Hill-dwellers were the center of attraction, Brick suddenly wormed out of his jacket, squirmed away from his captors, and dashed across the lot to the slip for which he had been originally headed when overtaken by Joe. Two or three of the gang shot over the fence after him in noisy pursuit. There was much barking and howling of back-yard dogs and clattering of shoes over sheds and boxes. Then there came a splashing of water, as though a barrel of it had been precipitated to the ground. Several minutes later the pursuers returned, very sheepish and very wet from the deluge presented them by the wily Brick, whose voice, high up in the air from some friendly housetop, could be heard defiantly jeering them.

This event apparently disconcerted the leader of the gang, and just as he turned to Joe and Fred and Charley, a long and peculiar whistle came to their ears from the street—the warning signal, evidently, of a scout posted to keep a lookout. The next moment the scout himself came flying back to the main body, which was already beginning to retreat.

"Cops!" he panted.

Joe looked, and he saw two helmeted policemen approaching, with bright stars shining on their breasts.

"Let's get out of this," he whispered to Fred and Charley.

The gang had already taken to flight, and they blocked the boys' retreat in one quarter, and in another they saw the policemen advancing. So they took to their heels in the direction of Brick Simpson's slip, the policemen hot after them and yelling bravely for them to halt.

But young feet are nimble, and young feet when frightened become something more than nimble, and the boys were first over the fence and plunging wildly through a maze of back yards. They soon found that the policemen were discreet. Evidently they had had experiences in slips, and they were satisfied to give over the chase at the first fence.

No street-lamps shed their light here, and the boys blundered along through the blackness with their hearts in their mouths. In one yard, filled with mountains of crates and fruit-boxes, they were lost for a quarter of an hour. Feel and quest about as they would, they encountered nothing but endless heaps of boxes. From this wilderness they finally emerged by way of a shed roof, only to fall into another yard, cumbered with countless empty chicken-coops.

Farther on they came upon the contrivance which had soaked Brick Simpson's pursuers with water. It was a cunning arrangement. Where the slip led through a fence with a board missing, a long slat was so arranged that the ignorant wayfarer could not fail to strike against it. This slat was the spring of the trap. A light touch upon it was sufficient to disconnect a heavy stone from a barrel perched overhead and nicely balanced. The disconnecting of the stone permitted the barrel to turn over and spill its contents on the one beneath who touched the slat.

The boys examined the arrangement with keen appreciation. Luckily for them, the barrel was overturned, or they too would have received a ducking, for Joe, who was in advance, had blundered against the slat.

"I wonder if this is Simpson's back yard?" he queried softly.

"It must be," Fred concluded, "or else the back yard of some member of his gang."

Charley put his hands warningly on both their arms.

"Hist! What's that?" he whispered.

They crouched down on the ground. Not far away was the sound of some one moving about. Then they heard a noise of falling water, as from a faucet into a bucket. This was followed by steps boldly approaching. They crouched lower, breathless with apprehension.

A dark form passed by within arm's-reach and mounted on a box to the fence. It was Brick himself, resetting the trap. They heard him arrange the slat and stone, then right the barrel and empty into it a couple of buckets of water. As he came down from the box to go after more water, Joe sprang upon him, tripped him up, and held him to the ground.

"Don't make any noise," he said. "I want you to listen to me."

"Oh, it 's you, is it?" Simpson replied, with such obvious relief in his voice as to make them feel relieved also. "Wot d' ye want here?"

"We want to get out of here," Joe said, "and the shortest way 's the best. There 's three of us, and you 're only one —"

"That 's all right, that 's all right," the gang-leader interrupted. "I 'd just as soon show you the way out as not. I ain't got nothin' 'gainst you. Come on an' follow me, an' don't step to the side, an' I 'll have you out in no time."

Several minutes later they dropped from the top of a high fence into a dark alley.

"Follow this to the street," Simpson directed; "turn to the right two blocks, turn to the right again for three, an' yer on Union. Tra-la-loo."

They said good-by, and as they started down the alley received the following advice:

"Nex' time you bring kites along, you 'd best leave 'em to home."

CHAPTER V

FOLLOWING Brick Simpson's directions, they came into Union
Street, and without further mishap gained
the Hill. From the brow they looked
down into the Pit, whence arose that
steady, indefinable hum which comes from
crowded human places.

"I 'll never go down there again, not
as long as I live," Fred said with a great
deal of savagery in his voice. "I wonder
what became of the fireman."

"We 're lucky to get back with whole
skins," Joe cheered them philosophically.

"I guess we left our share, and you
more than yours," laughed Charley.

"Yes," Joe answered. "And I 've got

54

more trouble to face when I get home. Good night, fellows."

As he expected, the door on the side porch was locked, and he went around to the dining-room and entered like a burglar through a window. As he crossed the wide hall, walking softly toward the stairs, his father came out of the library. The surprise was mutual, and each halted aghast.

Joe felt a hysterical desire to laugh, for he thought that he knew precisely how he looked. In reality he looked far worse than he imagined. What Mr. Bronson saw was a boy with hat and coat covered with dirt, his whole face smeared with the stains of conflict, and, in particular, a badly swollen nose, a bruised eyebrow, a cut and swollen lip, a scratched cheek, knuckles still bleeding, and a shirt torn open from throat to waist.

"What does this mean, sir?" Mr. Bronson finally managed to articulate.

Joe stood speechless. How could he

tell, in one brief sentence, all the whole night's happenings? — for all that must be included in the explanation of what his luckless disarray meant.

"Have you lost your tongue?" Mr. Bronson demanded with an appearance of impatience.

"I 've— I 've—"

"Yes, yes," his father encouraged.

"I 've — well, I 've been down in the Pit," Joe succeeded in blurting out.

"I must confess that you look like it — very much like it indeed." Mr. Bronson spoke severely, but if ever by great effort he conquered a smile, that was the time. "I presume," he went on, "that you do not refer to the abiding-place of sinners, but rather to some definite locality in San Francisco. Am I right?"

Joe swept his arm in a descending gesture toward Union Street, and said: "Down there, sir."

"And who gave it that name?"

"I did," Joe answered, as though confessing to a specified crime.

"It 's most appropriate, I 'm sure, and denotes imagination. It could n't really be bettered. You must do well at school, sir, with your English."

This did not increase Joe's happiness, for English was the only study of which he did not have to feel ashamed.

And, while he stood thus a silent picture of misery and disgrace, Mr. Bronson looked upon him through the eyes of his own boyhood with an understanding which Joe could not have believed possible.

"However, what you need just now is not a discourse, but a bath and court-plaster and witch-hazel and cold-water bandages," Mr. Bronson said; "so to bed with you. You 'll need all the sleep you can get, and you 'll feel stiff and sore tomorrow morning, I promise you."

The clock struck one as Joe pulled the bedclothes around him ; and the next he knew he was being worried by a soft, insistent rapping, which seemed to continue through several centuries, until at last, unable to endure it longer, he opened his eyes and sat up.

The day was streaming in through the window — bright and sunshiny day. He stretched his arms to yawn; but a shooting pain darted through all the muscles, and his arms came down more rapidly than they had gone up. He looked at them with a bewildered stare, till suddenly the events of the night rushed in upon him, and he groaned.

The rapping still persisted, and he cried: "Yes, I hear. What time is it?"

"Eight o'clock," Bessie's voice came to him through the door. "Eight o'clock, and you 'll have to hurry if you don't want to be late for school."

"Goodness!" He sprang out of bed precipitately, groaned with the pain from all his stiff muscles, and collapsed slowly and carefully on a chair. "Why did n't you call me sooner?" he growled.

"Father said to let you sleep."

Joe groaned again, in another fashion.

Then his history-book caught his eye, and he groaned yet again and in still another fashion.

"All right," he called. "Go on. I 'll be down in a jiffy."

He did come down in fairly brief order; but if Bessie had watched him descend the stairs she would have been astounded at the remarkable caution he observed and at the twinges of pain that every now and then contorted his face. As it was, when she came upon him in the dining-room she uttered a frightened cry and ran over to him.

"What 's the matter, Joe?" she asked tremulously. "What has happened?"

"Nothing," he grunted, putting sugar on his porridge.

"But surely—" she began.

"Please don't bother me," he interrupted. "I 'm late, and I want to eat my breakfast."

And just then Mrs. Bronson caught Bessie's eye, and that young lady, still mystified, made haste to withdraw herself.

Joe was thankful to his mother for that, and thankful that she refrained from remarking upon his appearance. Father had told her; that was one thing sure. He could trust her not to worry him; it was never her way.

And, meditating in this way, he hurried through with his solitary breakfast, vaguely conscious in an uncomfortable way that his mother was fluttering anxiously about him. Tender as she always was, he noticed that she kissed him with unusual tenderness as he started out with his books swinging at the end of a strap; and he also noticed, as he turned the corner, that she was still looking after him through the window.

But of more vital importance than that, to him, was his stiffness and soreness. As he walked along, each step was an effort and a torment. Severely as the reflected sunlight from the cement side-

walk hurt his bruised eye, and severely
as his various wounds pained him, still
more severely did he suffer from his muscles and joints. He had never imagined
such stiffness. Each individual muscle in
his whole body protested when called upon
to move. His fingers were badly swollen,
and it was agony to clasp and unclasp
them; while his arms were sore from wrist
to elbow. This, he said to himself, was
caused by the many blows which he had
warded off from his face and body. He
wondered if Brick Simpson was in similar plight, and the thought of their mutual
misery made him feel a certain kinship for
that redoubtable young ruffian.

When he entered the school-yard he
quickly became aware that he was the
center of attraction for all eyes. The
boys crowded around in an awe-stricken
way, and even his classmates and those
with whom he was well acquainted looked
at him with a certain respect he had never
seen before.

CHAPTER VI

EXAMINATION DAY

IT was plain that Fred and Charley had spread the news of their descent into the Pit, and of their battle with the Simpson clan and the Fishes. He heard the nine-o'clock bell with feelings of relief, and passed into the school, a mark for admiring glances from all the boys. The girls, too, looked at him in a timid and fearful way — as they might have looked at Daniel when he came out of the lions' den, Joe thought, or at David after his battle with Goliath. It made him uncomfortable and painfully self-conscious, this hero-worshiping, and he wished heartily that they would look in some other direction for a change.

Examination Day

Soon they did look in another direction. While big sheets of foolscap were being distributed to every desk, Miss Wilson, the teacher (an austere-looking young woman who went through the world as though it were a refrigerator, and who, even on the warmest days in the classroom, was to be found with a shawl or cape about her shoulders), arose, and on the blackboard where all could see wrote the Roman numeral "I." Every eye, and there were fifty pairs of them, hung with expectancy upon her hand, and in the pause that followed the room was quiet as the grave.

Underneath the Roman numeral "I" she wrote: "(*a*) *What were the laws of Draco?* (*b*) *Why did an Athenian orator say that they were written 'not in ink, but in blood'?*"

Forty-nine heads bent down and forty-nine pens scratched lustily across as many sheets of foolscap. Joe's head alone remained up, and he regarded the blackboard with so blank a stare that Miss Wilson, glancing over her shoulder after having written "II," stopped to look at him. Then she wrote :

"(*a*) *How did the war between Athens and Megara, respecting the island of Salamis, bring about the reforms of Solon? (b) In what way did they differ from the laws of Draco?*"

She turned to look at Joe again. He was staring as blankly as ever.

"What is the matter, Joe?" she asked. "Have you no paper?"

"Yes, I have, thank you," he answered, and began moodily to sharpen a lead-pencil.

He made a fine point to it. Then he made a very fine point. Then, and with infinite patience, he proceeded to make it very much finer. Several of his classmates raised their heads inquiringly at the noise. But he did not notice. He was too absorbed in his pencil-sharpening and in thinking thoughts far away from both pencil-sharpening and Greek history.

"Of course you all understand that the examination papers are to be written with ink."

Miss Wilson addressed the class in general, but her eyes rested on Joe.

Just as it was about as fine as it could possibly be the point broke, and Joe began over again.

"I am afraid, Joe, that you annoy the class," Miss Wilson said in final desperation.

He put the pencil down, closed the knife with a snap, and returned to his blank staring at the blackboard. What did he know about Draco? or Solon? or the rest of the Greeks? It was a flunk, and that was all there was to it. No need for him to look at the rest of the questions, and even if he did know the answers to two or three, there was no use in writing them down. It would not prevent the flunk. Besides, his arm hurt him too much to write. It hurt his eyes to look at the blackboard, and his eyes hurt even when they were closed; and it seemed positively to hurt him to think.

So the forty-nine pens scratched on in a race after Miss Wilson, who was covering the blackboard with question after question; and he listened to the scratching, and watched the questions growing under her chalk, and was very miserable indeed. His head seemed whirling around. It ached inside and was sore outside, and he did not seem to have any control of it at all.

He was beset with memories of the Pit, like scenes from some monstrous nightmare, and, try as he would, he could not dispel them. He would fix his mind and eyes on Miss Wilson's face, who was now sitting at her desk, and even as he looked at her the face of Brick Simpson, impudent and pugnacious, would arise before him. It was of no use. He felt sick and sore and tired and worthless. There

was nothing to be done but flunk. And
when, after an age of waiting, the papers
were collected, his went in a blank, save
for his name, the name of the examination,
and the date, which were written across
the top.

After a brief interval, more papers were
given out, and the examination in arithmetic began. He did not trouble himself
to look at the questions. Ordinarily he
might have pulled through such an examination, but in his present state of mind
and body he knew it was impossible. He
contented himself with burying his face
in his hands and hoping for the noon
hour. Once, lifting his eyes to the clock,
he caught Bessie looking anxiously at
him across the room from the girls' side.
This but added to his discomfort. Why
was she bothering him? No need for her
to trouble. She was bound to pass. Then
why could n't she leave him alone? So
he gave her a particularly glowering look
and buried his face in his hands again.

Nor did he lift it till the twelve-o'clock gong rang, when he handed in a second blank paper and passed out with the boys.

Fred and Charley and he usually ate lunch in a corner of the yard which they had arrogated to themselves; but this day, by some remarkable coincidence, a score of other boys had elected to eat their lunches on the same spot. Joe surveyed them with disgust. In his present condition he did not feel inclined to receive hero-worship. His head ached too much, and he was troubled over his failure in the examinations; and there were more to come in the afternoon.

He was angry with Fred and Charley. They were chattering like magpies over the adventures of the night (in which, however, they did not fail to give him chief credit), and they conducted themselves in quite a patronizing fashion toward their awed and admiring schoolmates. But every attempt to make Joe talk was a failure. He grunted and gave short answers, and said "yes" and "no" to questions asked with the intention of drawing him out.

He was longing to get away somewhere by himself, to throw himself down some place on the green grass and forget his aches and pains and troubles. He got up to go and find such a place, and found half a dozen of his following tagging after him. He wanted to turn around and scream at them to leave him alone, but his pride restrained him. A great wave of disgust and despair swept over him, and then an idea flashed through his mind. Since he was sure to flunk in his examinations, why endure the afternoon's torture, which could not but be worse than the morning's? And on the impulse of the moment he made up his mind.

He walked straight on to the school-yard gate and passed out. Here his worshipers halted in wonderment, but he kept on to the corner and out of sight. For some time he wandered along aimlessly, till he came to the tracks of a cable road. A down-town car happening to stop to let off passengers, he stepped aboard and ensconced himself in an outside corner seat. The next thing he was aware of, the car was swinging around on its turn-table and he was hastily scrambling off. The big ferry building stood before him. Seeing and hearing nothing, he had been carried through the heart of the business section of San Francisco.

He glanced up at the tower clock on top of the ferry building. It was ten minutes after one — time enough to catch the quarter-past-one boat. That decided him, and without the least idea in the world as to where he was going, he paid ten cents for a ticket, passed through the gate, and was soon speeding across the bay to the pretty city of Oakland.

In the same aimless and unwitting fashion, he found himself, an hour later, sitting on the string-piece of the Oakland city wharf and leaning his aching head against a friendly timber. From where he sat he could look down upon the decks of a number of small sailing-craft. Quite a crowd of curious idlers had collected to look at them, and Joe found himself growing interested.

There were four boats, and from where he sat he could make out their names. The one directly beneath him had the name *Ghost* painted in large green letters on its stern. The other three, which lay beyond, were called respectively *La Caprice*, the *Oyster Queen*, and the *Flying Dutchman*.

Each of these boats had cabins built amidships, with short stovepipes projecting through the roofs, and from the pipe of the *Ghost* smoke was ascending. The cabin doors were open and the roof-slide pulled back, so that Joe could look inside and observe the inmate, a young fellow of nineteen or twenty who was engaged just then in cooking. He was clad in long sea-boots which reached the hips, blue overalls, and dark woolen shirt. The sleeves, rolled back to the elbows, disclosed sturdy, sun-bronzed arms, and when the young fellow looked up his face proved to be equally bronzed and tanned.

The aroma of coffee arose to Joe's nose, and from a light iron pot came the unmistakable smell of beans nearly done. The cook placed a frying-pan on the stove, wiped it around with a piece of suet when it had heated, and tossed in a thick chunk of beefsteak. While he worked he talked with a companion on deck, who was busily engaged in filling a bucket overside and flinging the salt water over heaps of oysters that lay on the deck. This completed, he covered the oysters with wet sacks, and went into the cabin, where a place was set for him on a tiny table, and where the cook served the dinner and joined him in eating it.

Examination Day

All the romance of Joe's nature stirred at the sight. That was life. They were living, and gaining their living, out in the free open, under the sun and sky, with the sea rocking beneath them, and the wind blowing on them, or the rain falling on them, as the chance might be. Each day and every day he sat in a room, pent up with fifty more of his kind, racking his brains and cramming dry husks of knowledge, while they were doing all this, living glad and careless and happy, rowing boats and sailing, and cooking their own food, and certainly meeting with adventures such as one only dreams of in the crowded school-room.

Joe sighed. He felt that he was made for this sort of life and not for the life of a scholar. As a scholar he was undeniably a failure. He had flunked in his examinations, while at that very moment, he knew, Bessie was going triumphantly home, her last examination over and done, and with credit. Oh, it was not to

be borne ! His father was wrong in
sending him to school. That might be
well enough for boys who were inclined
to study, but it was manifest that he
was not so inclined. There were more
careers in life than that of the schools.
Men had gone down to the sea in the
lowest capacity, and risen in great-
ness, and owned great fleets, and done
great deeds, and left their names on the
pages of time. And why not he, Joe
Bronson?

He closed his eyes and felt immensely
sorry for himself; and when he opened
his eyes again he found that he had
been asleep, and that the sun was sinking
fast.

It was after dark when he arrived
home, and he went straight to his room
and to bed without meeting any one. He
sank down between the cool sheets with
a sigh of satisfaction at the thought that,
come what would, he need no longer
worry about his history. Then another

and unwelcome thought obtruded itself, and he knew that the next school term would come, and that six months thereafter, another examination in the same history awaited him.

CHAPTER VII

FATHER AND SON

ON the following morning, after breakfast, Joe was summoned to the library by his father, and he went in almost with a feeling of gladness that the suspense of waiting was over. Mr. Bronson was standing by the window. A great chattering of sparrows outside seemed to have attracted his attention. Joe joined him in looking out, and saw a fledgeling sparrow on the grass, tumbling ridiculously about in its efforts to stand on its feeble baby legs. It had fallen from the nest in the rose-bush that climbed over the window, and the two parent sparrows were wild with anxiety over its plight.

"It's a way young birds have," Mr. Bronson remarked, turning to Joe with a serious smile; "and I dare say you are on the verge of a somewhat similar predicament, my boy," he went on. "I am afraid things have reached a crisis, Joe. I have watched it coming on for a year now — your poor scholarship, your carelessness and inattention, your constant desire to be out of the house and away in search of adventures of one sort or another."

He paused, as though expecting a reply; but Joe remained silent.

"I have given you plenty of liberty. I believe in liberty. The finest souls grow in such soil. So I have not hedged you in with endless rules and irksome restrictions. I have asked little of you, and you have come and gone pretty much as you pleased. In a way, I have put you on your honor, made you largely your own master, trusting to your sense of right to restrain you from going wrong and at least to keep you up in your studies. And you have failed me. What do you want me to do? Set you certain bounds and time-limits? Keep a watch over you? Compel you by main strength to go through your books?

"I have here a note," Mr. Bronson said after another pause, in which he picked up an envelop from the table and drew forth a written sheet.

Joe recognized the stiff and uncompromising scrawl of Miss Wilson, and his heart sank.

His father began to read:

"Listlessness and carelessness have characterized his term's work, so that when the examinations came he was wholly unprepared. In neither history nor arithmetic did he attempt to answer a question, passing in his papers perfectly blank. These examinations took place in the morning. In the afternoon he did not take the trouble even to appear for the remainder."

Mr. Bronson ceased reading and looked up.

"Where were you in the afternoon?" he asked.

"I went across on the ferry to Oakland," Joe answered, not caring to offer his aching head and body in extenuation.

"That is what is called 'playing hooky,' is it not?"

"Yes, sir," Joe answered.

"The night before the examinations, instead of studying, you saw fit to wander away and involve yourself in a disgraceful fight with hoodlums. I did not say anything at the time. In my heart I think I might almost have forgiven you that, if you had done well in your school-work."

Joe had nothing to say. He knew that there was his side to the story, but he felt that his father did not understand, and that there was little use of telling him.

"The trouble with you, Joe, is carelessness and lack of concentration. What you need is what I have not given you, and that is rigid discipline. I have been debating for some time upon the advisability of sending you to some military school, where your tasks will be set for you, and what you do every moment in the twenty-four hours will be determined for you—"

"Oh, father, you don't understand, you can't understand!" Joe broke forth at last. "I try to study—I honestly try to study; but somehow—I don't know how—I can't study. Perhaps I am a failure. Perhaps I am not made for study. I want to go out into the world. I want to see life—to live. I don't want any military academy; I 'd sooner go to sea—anywhere where I can do something and be something."

Mr. Bronson looked at him kindly. "It is only through study that you can hope to do something and be something in the world," he said.

Joe threw up his hand with a gesture of despair.

"I know how you feel about it," Mr.

Bronson went on; "but you are only a boy, very much like that young sparrow we were watching. If at home you have not sufficient control over yourself to study, then away from home, out in the world which you think is calling to you, you will likewise not have sufficient control over yourself to do the work of that world.

"But I am willing, Joe, I am willing, after you have finished high school and before you go into the university, to let you out into the world for a time."

"Let me go now?" Joe asked impulsively.

"No; it is too early. You have n't your wings yet. You are too unformed, and your ideals and standards are not yet thoroughly fixed."

"But I shall not be able to study," Joe threatened. "I know I shall not be able to study."

Mr. Bronson consulted his watch and arose to go. "I have not made up my mind yet," he said. "I do not know what I shall do—whether I shall give you another trial at the public school or send you to a military academy."

He stopped a moment at the door and looked back. "But remember this, Joe," he said. "I am not angry with you; I am more grieved and hurt. Think it over, and tell me this evening what you intend to do."

His father passed out, and Joe heard the front door close after him. He leaned back in the big easy-chair and closed his eyes. A military school! He feared such an institution as the animal fears a trap. No, he would certainly never go to such a place. And as for public school— He sighed deeply at the thought of it. He was given till evening to make up his mind as to what he intended to do. Well, he knew what he would do, and he did not have to wait till evening to find it out.

He got up with a determined look on his face, put on his hat, and went out the front door. He would show his father that he could do his share of the world's work, he thought as he walked along — he would show him.

By the time he reached the school he had his whole plan worked out definitely. Nothing remained but to put it through. It was the noon hour, and he passed in to his room and packed up his books unnoticed. Coming out through the yard, he encountered Fred and Charley.

"What's up?" Charley asked.

"Nothing," Joe grunted.

"What are you doing there?"

"Taking my books home, of course. What did you suppose I was doing?"

"Come, come," Fred interposed. "Don't be so mysterious. I don't see why you can't tell us what has happened."

"You'll find out soon enough," Joe said significantly — more significantly than he had intended.

And, for fear that he might say more, he turned his back on his astonished chums and hurried away. He went straight home and to his room, where he busied himself at once with putting everything in order. His clothes he hung carefully away, changing the suit he had on for an older one. From his bureau he selected a couple of changes of underclothing, a couple of cotton shirts, and half a dozen pairs of socks. To these he added as many handkerchiefs, a comb, and a tooth-brush.

When he had bound the bundle in stout wrapping-paper he contemplated it with satisfaction. Then he went over to his desk and took from a small inner compartment his savings for some months, which amounted to several dollars. This sum he had been keeping for the Fourth of July, but he thrust it into his pocket with hardly a regret. Then he pulled a writing-pad over to him, sat down and wrote:

Don't look for me. I am a failure and I am going away to sea. Don't worry about me. I

am all right and able to take care of myself. I
shall come back some day, and then you will all
be proud of me. Good-by, papa, and mama, and
Bessie.   JOE.

This he left lying on his desk where it
could easily be seen. He tucked the
bundle under his arm, and, with a last
farewell look at the room, stole out.

PART II

CHAPTER VIII

'FRISCO KID was discontented — discontented and disgusted. This would have seemed impossible to the boys who fished from the dock above and envied him greatly. True, they wore cleaner and better clothes, and were blessed with fathers and mothers; but his was the free floating life of the bay, the domain of moving adventure, and the companionship of men — theirs the rigid discipline and dreary sameness of home life. They did not dream that 'Frisco Kid ever looked up at them from the cockpit of the *Dazzler* and in turn envied them just those things which sometimes were the most distasteful to them and from which they suffered to repletion. Just as the romance of adventure sang its siren song in their ears and whispered vague messages of strange lands and lusty deeds, so the delicious mysteries of home enticed 'Frisco Kid's roving fancies, and his brightest day-dreams were of the things he knew not — brothers, sisters, a father's counsel, a mother's kiss.

He frowned, got up from where he had been sunning himself on top of the *Dazzler's* cabin, and kicked off his heavy rubber boots. Then he stretched himself on the narrow side-deck and dangled his feet in the cool salt water.

"Now that 's freedom," thought the boys who watched him. Besides, those long sea-boots, reaching to the hips and buckled to the leather strap about the waist, held a strange and wonderful fascination for them. They did not know that 'Frisco Kid did not possess such things as shoes — that the boots were an old pair of Pete Le Maire's and were three sizes too large for him. Nor could they guess how uncomfortable they were to wear on a hot summer day.

The cause of 'Frisco Kid's discontent was those very boys who sat on the string-piece and admired him; but his disgust was the result of quite another event. The *Dazzler* was short one in its crew, and he had to do more work than was justly his share. He did not mind the cooking, nor the washing down of the decks and the pumping; but when it came to the paint-scrubbing and dish-washing he rebelled. He felt that he had earned the right to be exempt from such scullion work. That was all the green boys were fit for, while he could make or take in sail, lift anchor, steer, and make landings.

"Stan' from un'er!" Pete Le Maire or "French Pete," captain of the *Dazzler* and lord and master of 'Frisco Kid, threw a bundle into the cockpit and came aboard by the starboard rigging.

"Come! Queeck!" he shouted to the boy who owned the bundle and who now hesitated on the dock. It was a good fifteen feet to the deck of the sloop, and he could not reach the steel stay by which he must descend.

"Now! One, two, three!" the Frenchman counted good-naturedly, after the manner of captains when their crews are short-handed.

The boy swung his body into space and gripped the rigging. A moment later he struck the deck, his hands tingling warmly from the friction.

"Kid, dis is ze new sailor. I make your acquaintance." French Pete smirked and bowed, and stood aside. "Mistaire Sho Bronson," he added as an afterthought.

The two boys regarded each other silently for a moment. They were evidently about the same age, though the stranger looked the heartier and stronger of the two. 'Frisco Kid put out his hand, and they shook.

"So you 're thinking of tackling the water, eh?" he said.

Joe Bronson nodded and glanced curiously about him before answering: "Yes; I think the bay life will suit me for a while, and then, when I 've got used to it, I 'm going to sea in the forecastle."

"In the what?"

"In the forecastle—the place where the sailors live," he explained, flushing and feeling doubtful of his pronunciation.

"Oh, the fo'c'sle. Know anything about going to sea?"

"Yes — no; that is, except what I 've read."

'Frisco Kid whistled, turned on his heel in a lordly manner, and went into the cabin.

"Going to sea," he chuckled to himself as he built the fire and set about cooking supper; "in the 'forecastle,' too; and thinks he 'll like it."

In the meanwhile French Pete was showing the newcomer about the sloop as though he were a guest. Such affability and charm did he display that 'Frisco Kid, popping his head up through the scuttle to call them to supper, nearly choked in his effort to suppress a grin.

Joe Bronson enjoyed that supper. The food was rough but good, and the smack of the salt air and the sea-fittings around him gave zest to his appetite. The cabin was clean and snug, and, though not large, the accommodations surprised him. Every bit of space was utilized. The table swung to the centerboard-case on hinges, so that when not in use it actually occupied no room at all. On either side and partly under the deck were two bunks. The blankets were rolled back, and the boys sat on the well-scrubbed bunk boards while they ate. A swinging sea-lamp of brightly polished brass gave them light, which in the daytime could be obtained through the four deadeyes, or small

'Frisco Kid and Joe regard each other
silently for a moment

round panes of heavy glass which were fitted into the walls of the cabin. On one side of the door was the stove and wood-box, on the other the cupboard. The front end of the cabin was ornamented with a couple of rifles and a shot-gun, while exposed by the rolled-back blankets of French Pete's bunk was a cartridge-lined belt carrying a brace of revolvers.

It all seemed like a dream to Joe. Countless times he had imagined scenes somewhat similar to this; but here he was right in the midst of it, and already it seemed as though he had known his two companions for years. French Pete was smiling genially at him across the board. It really was a villainous counte-nance, but to Joe it seemed only weather-beaten. 'Frisco Kid was describing to him, between mouthfuls, the last sou'-easter the *Dazzler* had weathered, and Joe experienced an increasing awe for this boy who had lived so long upon the water and knew so much about it.

The captain, however, drank a glass of wine, and topped it off with a second and a third, and then, a vicious flush lighting his swarthy face, stretched out on top of his blankets, where he soon was snoring loudly.

"Better turn in and get a couple of hours' sleep," 'Frisco Kid said kindly, pointing Joe's bunk out to him. "We'll most likely be up the rest of the night."

Joe obeyed, but he could not fall asleep so readily as the others. He lay with his eyes wide open, watching the hands of the alarm-clock that hung in the cabin, and thinking how quickly event had followed event in the last twelve hours. Only that very morning he had been a school-boy, and now he was a sailor, shipped on the *Dazzler* and bound he knew not whither. His fifteen years increased to twenty at the thought of it, and he felt every inch a man — a sailorman at that. He wished Charley and Fred could see him now. Well, they would hear of it soon enough. He could see them talking it over, and the other boys crowding around. "Who?" "Oh, Joe Bronson; he's gone to sea. Used to chum with us."

Joe pictured the scene proudly. Then he softened at the thought of his mother worrying, but hardened again at the recollection of his father. Not that his father was not good and kind; but he did not understand boys, Joe thought. That was where the trouble lay. Only that morning he had said that the world was n't a play-ground, and that the boys who thought it was were liable to make sore mistakes and be glad to get home again. Well, *he* knew that there was plenty of hard work and rough experience in the world; but *he* also thought boys had some rights. He'd show him he could take care of himself; and, anyway, he could write home after he got settled down to his new life.

CHAPTER IX

ABOARD THE DAZZLER

A SKIFF grazed the side of the *Dazzler* softly and interrupted Joe's reveries. He wondered why he had not heard the sound of the oars in the rowlocks. Then two men jumped over the cockpit-rail and came into the cabin.

"Bli' me, if 'ere they ain't snoozin'," said the first of the newcomers, deftly rolling 'Frisco Kid out of his blankets with one hand and reaching for the wine-bottle with the other.

French Pete put his head up on the other side of the centerboard, his eyes heavy with sleep, and made them welcome.

"'Oo 's this?" asked the Cockney,

as he was called, smacking his lips over the wine and rolling Joe out upon the floor. "Passenger?"

"No, no," French Pete made haste to answer. "Ze new sailorman. Vaire good boy."

"Good boy or not, he 's got to keep his tongue atween his teeth," growled the second newcomer, who had not yet spoken, glaring fiercely at Joe.

"I say," queried the other man, "'ow does 'e whack up on the loot? I 'ope as me and Bill 'ave a square deal."

"Ze *Dazzler* she take one share—what you call—one third; den we split ze rest in five shares. Five men, five shares. Vaire good."

French Pete insisted in excited gibberish that the *Dazzler* had the right to have three men in its crew, and appealed to 'Frisco Kid to bear him out. But the latter left them to fight it over by themselves, and proceeded to make hot coffee.

It was all Greek to Joe, except he knew

that he was in some way the cause of the quarrel. In the end French Pete had his way, and the newcomers gave in after much grumbling. After they had drunk their coffee, all hands went on deck.

"Just stay in the cockpit and keep out of their way," 'Frisco Kid whispered to Joe. "I'll teach you about the ropes and everything when we ain't in a hurry."

Joe's heart went out to him in sudden gratitude, for the strange feeling came to him that of those on board, to 'Frisco Kid, and to 'Frisco Kid only, could he look for help in time of need. Already a dislike for French Pete was growing up within him. Why, he could not say; he just simply felt it.

A creaking of blocks for'ard, and the huge mainsail loomed above him in the night. Bill cast off the bowline, the Cockney followed suit with the stern, 'Frisco Kid gave her the jib as French Pete jammed up the tiller, and the *Dazzler* caught the breeze, heeling over for mid-channel. Joe heard talk of not putting up the side-lights, and of keeping a sharp lookout, though all he could comprehend was that some law of navigation was being violated.

The water-front lights of Oakland began to slip past. Soon the stretches of docks and the shadowy ships began to be broken by dim sweeps of marshland, and Joe knew that they were heading out for San Francisco Bay. The wind was blowing from the north in mild squalls, and the *Dazzler* cut noiselessly through the landlocked water.

"Where are we going?" Joe asked the Cockney, in an endeavor to be friendly and at the same time satisfy his curiosity.

"Oh, my pardner 'ere, Bill, we 're goin' to take a cargo from 'is factory," that worthy airily replied.

Joe thought he was rather a funny-looking individual to own a factory; but, conscious that even stranger things might be found in this new world he was entering, he said nothing. He had already exposed himself to 'Frisco Kid in the matter of his pronunciation of "fo'c'sle," and he had no desire further to advertise his ignorance.

A little after that he was sent in to blow out the cabin lamp. The *Dazzler* tacked about and began to work in toward the north shore. Everybody kept silent, save for occasional whispered questions and answers which passed between Bill and the captain. Finally the sloop was run into the wind, and the jib and mainsail lowered cautiously.

" Short hawse," French Pete whispered to 'Frisco Kid, who went for'ard and dropped the anchor, paying out the slightest quantity of slack.

The *Dazzler's* skiff was brought alongside, as was also the small boat in which the two strangers had come aboard.

" See that that cub don't make a fuss," Bill commanded in an undertone, as he joined his partner in his own boat.

"Can you row?" 'Frisco Kid asked as they got into the other boat.

Joe nodded his head.

"Then take these oars, and don't make a racket."

"'Frisco Kid took the second pair, while French Pete steered. Joe noticed that the oars were muffled with sennit, and that even the rowlock sockets were protected with leather. It was impossible to make a noise except by a mis-stroke, and Joe had learned to row on Lake Merrit well enough to avoid that. They followed in the wake of the first boat, and, glancing aside, he saw they were running along the length of a pier which jutted out from the land. A couple of ships, with riding-lanterns burning brightly, were moored to it, but they kept just beyond the edge of the light. He stopped rowing at the whispered command of 'Frisco Kid. Then the boats grounded like ghosts on a tiny beach, and they clambered out.

Joe followed the men, who picked their way carefully up a twenty-foot bank. At the top he found himself on a narrow railway track which ran between huge piles of rusty scrap-iron. These piles, separated by tracks, extended in every direction he could not tell how far, though in the distance he could see the vague outlines of some great factory-like building. The men began to carry loads of the iron down to the beach, and French Pete, gripping him by the arm and again warning him not to make any noise, told him to do likewise. At the beach they turned their burdens over to 'Frisco Kid, who loaded them, first in the one skiff and then in the other. As the boats settled under the weight, he kept pushing them farther and farther out, in order that they should keep clear of the bottom.

Joe worked away steadily, though he could not help marveling at the queerness of the whole business. Why should there be such a mystery about it? and why such care taken to maintain silence? He had just begun to ask himself these questions, and a horrible suspicion was forming itself in his mind, when he heard the hoot of an owl from the direction of the beach. Wondering at an owl being in so unlikely a place, he stooped to gather a fresh load of iron. But suddenly a man sprang out of the gloom, flashing a dark lantern full upon him. Blinded by the light, he staggered back. Then a revolver in the man's hand went off like the roar of a cannon. All Joe realized was that he was being shot at, while his legs manifested an overwhelming desire to get away. Even if he had so wished, he could not very well have stayed to explain to the excited man with the smoking revolver. So he took to his heels for the beach, colliding with another man with a dark lantern who came running around the end of one of the piles of iron. This second man quickly regained his feet, and peppered away at Joe as he flew down the bank.

He dashed out into the water for the boat. French Pete at the bow-oars and 'Frisco Kid at the stroke had the skiff's nose pointed seaward and were calmly awaiting his arrival. They had their oars ready for the start, but they held them quietly at rest, for all that both men on the bank had begun to fire at them. The other skiff lay closer inshore, partially aground. Bill was trying to shove it off, and was calling on the Cockney to lend a hand; but that gentleman had lost his head completely, and came floundering through the water hard after Joe. No sooner had Joe climbed in over the stern than he followed him. This extra weight on the stern of the heavily loaded craft nearly swamped them. As it was, a dangerous quantity of water was shipped. In the meantime the men on the bank had reloaded their pistols and opened fire again, this time with better aim. The alarm had spread. Voices and cries could be heard from the ships on the pier, along which men were running. In the distance a police whistle was being frantically blown.

"Get out!" 'Frisco Kid shouted. "You ain't a-going to sink us if I know it. Go and help your pardner."

But the Cockney's teeth were chattering with fright, and he was too unnerved to move or speak.

"T'row ze crazy man out!" French Pete ordered from the bow. At this moment a bullet shattered an oar in his hand, and he coolly proceeded to ship a spare one.

"Give us a hand, Joe," 'Frisco Kid commanded.

Joe understood, and together they seized the terror-stricken creature and flung him overboard. Two or three bullets splashed about him as he came to the surface, just in time to be picked up by Bill, who had at last succeeded in getting clear.

"Now!" French Pete called, and a few

109

strokes into the darkness quickly took
them out of the zone of fire.

So much water had been shipped that
the light skiff was in danger of sinking
at any moment. While the other two
rowed, and by the Frenchman's orders,
Joe began to throw out the iron. This
saved them for the time being. But just
as they swept alongside the *Dazzler* the
skiff lurched, shoved a side under, and
turned turtle, sending the remainder of
the iron to bottom. Joe and 'Frisco
Kid came up side by side, and together
they clambered aboard with the skiff's
painter in tow. French Pete had already
arrived, and now helped them out.

By the time they had canted the water
out of the swamped boat, Bill and his
partner appeared on the scene. All hands
worked rapidly, and, almost before Joe
could realize, the mainsail and jib had
been hoisted, the anchor broken out, and
the *Dazzler* was leaping down the channel. Off a bleak piece of marshland Bill

and the Cockney said good-by and cast loose in their skiff. French Pete, in the cabin, bewailed their bad luck in various languages, and sought consolation in the wine-bottle.

CHAPTER X

THE wind freshened as they got clear of the land, and soon the *Dazzler* was heeling it with her lee deck buried and the water churning by, half-way up the cockpit-rail. Side-lights had been hung out. 'Frisco Kid was steering, and by his side sat Joe, pondering over the events of the night.

He could no longer blind himself to the facts. His mind was in a whirl of apprehension. If he had done wrong, he reasoned, he had done it through ignorance; and he did not feel shame for the past so much as he did fear for the future. His companions were thieves and robbers — the bay pirates, of whose wild deeds he had heard vague tales. And here he was, right in the midst of them, already possessing information which could send them to State's prison. This very fact, he knew, would force them to keep a sharp watch upon him and so lessen his chances of escape. But escape he would, at the very first opportunity.

At this point his thoughts were interrupted by a sharp squall, which hurled the *Dazzler* over till the sea rushed inboard. 'Frisco Kid luffed quickly, at the same time slacking off the main-sheet. Then, single-handed,— for French Pete remained below,— and with Joe looking idly on, he proceeded to reef down.

The squall which had so nearly capsized the *Dazzler* was of short duration, but it marked the rising of the wind, and soon puff after puff was shrieking down upon them out of the north. The mainsail was spilling the wind, and slapping and thrashing about till it seemed it would tear itself to pieces. The sloop was rolling wildly in the quick sea which had come up. Everything was in confusion; but even Joe's untrained eye showed him that it was an orderly confusion. He could see that 'Frisco Kid knew just what to do and just how to do it. As he watched him he learned a lesson, the lack of which has made failures of the lives of many men — *the value of knowledge of one's own capacities*. 'Frisco Kid knew what he was able to do, and because of this he had confidence in himself. He was cool and self-possessed, working hurriedly but not carelessly. There was no bungling. Every reef-point was drawn down to stay. Other accidents might occur, but the next squall, or the next forty squalls, would not carry one of those reef-knots away.

He called Joe for'ard to help stretch the mainsail by means of swinging on the peak and throat-halyards. To lay out on the long bowsprit and put a single reef in the jib was a slight task compared with what had been already accomplished; so a few moments later they were again in the cockpit. Under the other lad's directions, Joe flattened down the jib-sheet, and, going into the cabin, let down a foot or so of centerboard. The excitement of the struggle had chased all unpleasant thoughts from his mind. Patterning after the other boy, he had retained his coolness. He had executed his orders without fumbling, and at the same time without undue slowness. Together they had exerted their puny strength in the face of violent nature, and together they had outwitted her.

He came back to where his companion stood at the tiller steering, and he felt proud of him and of himself; and when he read the unspoken praise in 'Frisco Kid's eyes he blushed like a girl at her first compliment. But the next instant the thought flashed across him that this boy was a thief, a common thief; and he instinctively recoiled. His whole life had been sheltered from the harsher things of the world. His reading, which had been of the best, had laid a premium upon honesty and uprightness, and he had learned to look with abhorrence upon the criminal classes. So he drew a little away from 'Frisco Kid and remained silent. But 'Frisco Kid, devoting all his energies to the handling of the sloop, had no time in which to remark this sudden change of feeling on the part of his companion.

But there was one thing Joe found in himself that surprised him. While the thought of 'Frisco Kid being a thief was repulsive to him, 'Frisco Kid himself was not. Instead of feeling an honest desire to shun him, he felt drawn toward him. He could not help liking him, though he knew not why. Had he been a little older he would have understood that it was the lad's good qualities which appealed to him — his coolness and self-reliance, his manliness and bravery, and a certain kindliness and sympathy in his nature. As it was, he thought it his own natural badness which prevented him from disliking 'Frisco Kid; but, while he felt shame at his own weakness, he could not smother the warm regard which he felt growing up for this particular bay pirate.

"Take in two or three feet on the skiff's painter," commanded 'Frisco Kid, who had an eye for everything.

The skiff was towing with too long a painter, and was behaving very badly. Every once in a while it would hold back till the tow-rope tautened, then come leaping ahead and sheering and dropping slack till it threatened to shove its nose under the huge whitecaps which roared so hungrily on every hand. Joe climbed over the cockpit-rail to the slippery after-deck, and made his way to the bitt to which the skiff was fastened.

"Be careful," 'Frisco Kid warned, as a heavy puff struck the *Dazzler* and careened her dangerously over on her side. "Keep one turn round the bitt, and heave in on it when the painter slacks."

It was ticklish work for a greenhorn. Joe threw off all the turns save the last, which he held with one hand, while with the other he attempted to bring in on the painter. But at that instant it tightened with a tremendous jerk, the boat sheering sharply into the crest of a heavy sea. The rope slipped from his hands and began to fly out over the stern. He clutched it frantically, and was dragged after it over the sloping deck.

"Let her go! Let her go!" 'Frisco Kid shouted.

Joe let go just as he was on the verge of going overboard, and the skiff dropped rapidly astern. He glanced in a shame-faced way at his companion, expecting to be sharply reprimanded for his awkwardness. But 'Frisco Kid smiled good-naturedly.

"That 's all right," he said. "No bones broke and nobody overboard. Better to

lose a boat than a man any day; that's what
I say. Besides, I should n't have sent
you out there. And there 's no harm
done. We can pick it up all right. Go
in and drop some more centerboard,— a
couple of feet,— and then come out and
do what I tell you. But don't be in a
hurry. Take it easy and sure."

Joe dropped the centerboard and returned, to be stationed at the jib-sheet.

"Hard a-lee!" 'Frisco Kid cried, throwing the tiller down, and following it with
his body. "Cast off! That 's right. Now
lend a hand on the main-sheet!"

Together, hand over hand, they came
in on the reefed mainsail. Joe began to
warm up with the work. The *Dazzler*
turned on her heel like a race-horse, and
swept into the wind, her canvas snarling
and her sheets slatting like hail.

"Draw down the jib-sheet!"

Joe obeyed, and, the head-sail filling,
forced her off on the other tack. This
manœuver had turned French Pete's bunk

from the lee to the weather side, and rolled him out on the cabin floor, where he lay in a drunken stupor.

'Frisco Kid, with his back against the tiller and holding the sloop off that it might cover their previous course, looked at him with an expression of disgust, and muttered: "The dog! We could well go to the bottom, for all he 'd care or do!"

Twice they tacked, trying to go over the same ground; and then Joe discovered the skiff bobbing to windward in the star-lit darkness.

"Plenty of time," 'Frisco Kid cautioned, shooting the *Dazzler* into the wind toward it and gradually losing headway. "Now!"

Joe leaned over the side, grasped the trailing painter, and made it fast to the bitt. Then they tacked ship again and started on their way. Joe still felt ashamed for the trouble he had caused; but 'Frisco Kid quickly put him at ease.

"Oh, that 's nothing," he said. "Every-

body does that when they 're beginning.
Now some men forget all about the trouble they had in learning, and get mad when a greeny makes a mistake. I never do. Why, I remember —"

And then he told Joe of many of the mishaps which fell to him when, as a little lad, he first went on the water, and of some of the severe punishments for the same which were measured out to him. He had passed the running end of a lanyard over the tiller-neck, and as they talked they sat side by side and close against each other in the shelter of the cockpit.

"What place is that?" Joe asked, as they flew by a lighthouse blinking from a rocky headland.

"Goat Island. They 've got a naval training station for boys over on the other side, and a torpedo-magazine. There 's jolly good fishing, too—rock-cod. We 'll pass to the lee of it, and make across, and anchor in the shelter of Angel Island. There 's a quarantine station there. Then when French Pete gets sober we 'll know where he wants to go. You can turn in now and get some sleep. I can manage all right."

Joe shook his head. There had been too much excitement for him to feel in the least like sleeping. He could not bear to think of it with the *Dazzler* leaping and surging along and shattering the seas into clouds of spray on her weather bow. His clothes had half dried already, and he preferred to stay on deck and enjoy it.

The lights of Oakland had dwindled till they made only a hazy flare against the sky; but to the south the San Francisco lights, topping hills and sinking into valleys, stretched miles upon miles. Starting from the great ferry building, and passing on to Telegraph Hill, Joe was soon able to locate the principal places of the city. Somewhere over in that maze of light and shadow was the home of his father, and perhaps even now they were thinking and worrying about him; and over there Bessie was sleeping cozily, to wake up in the morning and wonder why her brother Joe did not come down to breakfast. Joe shivered. It was almost morning. Then slowly his head dropped over on 'Frisco Kid's shoulder and he was fast asleep.

CHAPTER XI

"COME! Wake up! We're going into anchor."

Joe roused with a start, bewildered at the unusual scene; for sleep had banished his troubles for the time being, and he knew not where he was. Then he remembered. The wind had dropped with the night. Beyond, the heavy after-sea was still rolling; but the *Dazzler* was creeping up in the shelter of a rocky island. The sky was clear, and the air had the snap and vigor of early morning about it. The rippling water was laughing in the rays of the sun just shouldering above the eastern sky-line. To the south lay Alcatraz Island, and from its gun-crowned heights a flourish of trumpets saluted the day. In the west the Golden Gate yawned between the Pacific Ocean and San Francisco Bay. A full-rigged ship, with her lightest canvas, even to the sky-sails, set, was coming slowly in on the flood-tide.

It was a pretty sight. Joe rubbed the sleep from his eyes and drank in the glory of it till 'Frisco Kid told him to go for'ard and make ready for dropping the anchor.

"Overhaul about fifty fathoms of chain," he ordered, "and then stand by." He eased the sloop gently into the wind, at the same time casting off the jib-sheet. "Let go the jib-halyards and come in on the downhaul!"

Joe had seen the manœuver performed the previous night, and so was able to carry it out with fair success.

"Now! Over with the mud-hook! Watch out for turns! Lively, now!"

The chain flew out with startling rapidity and brought the *Dazzler* to rest.

'Frisco Kid went for'ard to help, and together they lowered the mainsail, furled it in shipshape manner and made all fast with the gaskets, and put the crutches under the main-boom.

" Here 's a bucket," said 'Frisco Kid, as he passed him the article in question. " Wash down the decks, and don't be afraid of the water, nor of the dirt either. Here 's a broom. Give it what for, and have everything shining. When you get that done bail out the skiff. She opened her seams a little last night. I 'm going below to cook breakfast."

The water was soon slushing merrily over the deck, while the smoke pouring from the cabin stove carried a promise of good things to come. Time and again Joe lifted his head from his task to take in the scene. It was one to appeal to any healthy boy, and he was no exception. The romance of it stirred him strangely, and his happiness would have been complete could he have escaped remembering who and what his companions were. The thought of this, and of French Pete in his bleary sleep below, marred the beauty of the day. He had been unused to such things and was shocked at the harsh reality of life. But instead of hurting him, as it might a lad of weaker nature, it had the opposite effect. It strengthened his desire to be clean and strong, and to not be ashamed of himself in his own eyes. He glanced about him and sighed. Why could not men be honest and true? It seemed too bad that he must go away and leave all this; but the events of the night were strong upon him, and he knew that in order to be true to himself he must escape.

At this juncture he was called to breakfast. He discovered that 'Frisco Kid was as good a cook as he was a sailor, and made haste to do justice to the fare. There were mush and condensed milk, beefsteak and fried potatoes, and all topped off with good French bread, butter, and coffee. French Pete did not join them, though 'Frisco Kid attempted a couple of times to rouse him. He mumbled and grunted, half opened his bleared eyes, then fell to snoring again.

"Can't tell when he 's going to get those spells," 'Frisco Kid explained, when Joe, having finished washing dishes, came on deck. "Sometimes he won't get that way for a month, and others he won't be decent for a week at a stretch. Sometimes he 's good-natured, and sometimes he 's dangerous; so the best thing to do is to let him alone and keep out of his way; and don't cross him, for if you do there 's liable to be trouble.

"Come on; let 's take a swim," he added, abruptly changing the subject to one more agreeable. "Can you swim?"

Joe nodded.

"What 's that place?" he asked, as he poised before diving, pointing toward a sheltered beach on the island where there were several buildings and a large number of tents.

"Quarantine station. Lots of small-pox coming in now on the China steamers, and they make them go there till the doctors say they're safe to land. I tell you, they're strict about it, too. Why—"

Splash! Had 'Frisco Kid finished his sentence just then, instead of diving overboard, much trouble might have been saved to Joe. But he did not finish it, and Joe dived after him.

"I'll tell you what," 'Frisco Kid suggested half an hour later, while they clung to the bobstay preparatory to climbing out. "Let's catch a mess of fish for dinner, and then turn in and make up for the sleep we lost last night. What d' you say?"

They made a race to clamber aboard, but Joe was shoved over the side again. When he finally did arrive, the other lad had brought to light a pair of heavily leaded, large-hooked lines and a mackerel-keg of salt sardines.

"Bait," he said. "Just shove a whole

131

one on. They 're not a bit partic'lar.
Swallow the bait, hook and all, and go —
that 's their caper. The fellow that
does n't catch the first fish has to clean
'em.''

Both sinkers started on their long descent together, and seventy feet of line
whizzed out before they came to rest.
But at the instant his sinker touched the
bottom Joe felt the struggling jerks of a
hooked fish. As he began to haul in he
glanced at 'Frisco Kid and saw that he
too had evidently captured a finny prize.
The race between them was exciting.
Hand over hand the wet lines flashed inboard. But 'Frisco Kid was more expert,
and his fish tumbled into the cockpit first.
Joe's followed an instant later — a three-
pound rock-cod. He was wild with joy.
It was magnificent — the largest fish he
had ever landed or ever seen landed.
Over went the lines again, and up they
came with two mates of the ones already
captured. It was sport royal. Joe would

certainly have continued till he had fished the bay empty, had not 'Frisco Kid persuaded him to stop.

"We've got enough for three meals now," he said, "so there's no use in having them spoil. Besides, the more you catch the more you clean, and you'd better start in right away. I'm going to bed."

CHAPTER XII

JOE TRIES TO TAKE FRENCH LEAVE

JOE did not mind. In fact, he was glad he had not caught the first fish, for it helped out a little plan which had come to him while swimming. He threw the last cleaned fish into a bucket of water and glanced about him. The quarantine station was a bare half-mile away, and he could make out a soldier pacing up and down at sentry duty on the beach. Going into the cabin, he listened to the heavy breathing of the sleepers. He had to pass so close to 'Frisco Kid to get his bundle of clothes that he decided not to take it. Returning outside, he carefully pulled the skiff alongside, got aboard with a pair of oars, and cast off.

At first he rowed very gently in the direction of the station, fearing the chance of noise if he made undue haste. But gradually he increased the strength of his strokes till he had settled down to the regular stride. When he had covered half the distance he glanced about. Escape was sure now, for he knew, even if he were discovered, that it would be impossible for the *Dazzler* to get under way and head him off before he made the land and the protection of that man who wore the uniform of Uncle Sam's soldiers.

The report of a gun came to him from the shore, but his back was in that direction and he did not bother to turn around. A second report followed, and a bullet cut the water within a couple of feet of his oar-blade. This time he did turn around. The soldier on the beach was leveling his rifle at him for a third shot.

Joe was in a predicament, and a very tantalizing one at that. A few minutes of hard rowing would bring him to the beach and to safety; but on that beach, for some unaccountable reason, stood a United States soldier who persisted in firing at him. When Joe saw the gun aimed at him for the third time, he backed water hastily. As a result, the skiff came to a standstill, and the soldier, lowering his rifle, regarded him intently.

"I want to come ashore! Important!" Joe shouted out to him.

The man in uniform shook his head.

"But it's important, I tell you! Won't you let me come ashore?"

He took a hurried look in the direction of the *Dazzler*. The shots had evidently awakened French Pete, for the mainsail had been hoisted, and as he looked he saw the anchor broken out and the jib flung to the breeze.

"Can't land here!" the soldier shouted back. "Smallpox!"

"But I must!" he cried, choking down a half-sob and preparing to row.

"Then I'll shoot you," was the cheering response, and the rifle came to shoulder again.

Joe thought rapidly. The island was large. Perhaps there were no soldiers farther on, and if he only once got ashore he did not care how quickly they captured him. He might catch the smallpox, but even that was better than going back to the bay pirates. He whirled the skiff half about to the right, and threw all his strength against the oars. The cove was quite wide, and the nearest point which he must go around a good distance away. Had he been more of a sailor, he would have gone in the other direction for the opposite point, and thus had the wind on his pursuers. As it was, the *Dazzler* had a beam wind in which to overtake him.

It was nip and tuck for a while. The breeze was light and not very steady, so sometimes he gained and sometimes they. Once it freshened till the sloop was within a hundred yards of him, and then it dropped suddenly flat, the *Daz-*

zler's big mainsail flapping idly from side to side.

"Ah! you steal ze skiff, eh?" French Pete howled at him, running into the cabin for his rifle. "I fix you! You come back queeck, or I kill you!" But he knew the soldier was watching them from the shore, and did not dare to fire, even over the lad's head.

Joe did not think of this, for he, who had never been shot at in all his previous life, had been under fire twice in the last twenty-four hours. Once more or less could n't amount to much. So he pulled steadily away, while French Pete raved like a wild man, threatening him with all manner of punishments once he laid hands upon him again. To complicate matters, 'Frisco Kid waxed mutinous.

"Just you shoot him, and I 'll see you hung for it—see if I don't," he threatened. "You 'd better let him go. He 's a good boy and all right, and not raised for the dirty life you and I are leading."

French Pete headed the sloop towards
Joe in the skiff

"You too, eh!" the Frenchman shrieked, beside himself with rage. "Den I fix you, you rat!"

He made a rush for the boy, but 'Frisco Kid led him a lively chase from cockpit to bowsprit and back again. A sharp capful of wind arriving just then, French Pete abandoned the one chase for the other. Springing to the tiller and slacking away on the main-sheet,—for the wind favored,—he headed the sloop down upon Joe. The latter made one tremendous spurt, then gave up in despair and hauled in his oars. French Pete let go the main-sheet, lost steerageway as he rounded up alongside the motionless skiff, and dragged Joe out.

"Keep mum," 'Frisco Kid whispered to him while the irate Frenchman was busy fastening the painter. "Don't talk back. Let him say all he wants to, and keep quiet. It 'll be better for you."

But Joe's Anglo-Saxon blood was up, and he did not heed.

"Look here, Mr. French Pete, or whatever your name is," he commenced; "I
give you to understand that I want to
quit, and that I 'm going to quit. So
you 'd better put me ashore at once. If
you don't I 'll put you in prison, or my
name 's not Joe Bronson."

'Frisco Kid waited the outcome fearfully. French Pete was aghast. He was
being defied aboard his own vessel — and
by a boy! Never had such a thing been
heard of. He knew he was committing an
unlawful act in detaining him, but at the
same time he was afraid to let him go with
the information he had gathered concerning the sloop and its occupation. The boy
had spoken the unpleasant truth when he
said he could send him to prison. The
only thing for him to do was to bully
him.

"You will, eh?" His shrill voice rose
wrathfully. "Den you come too. You
row ze boat last-a night — answer me dat!
You steal ze iron — answer me dat! You

run away — answer me dat! And den you say you put me in jail? Bah!"

"But I did n't know," Joe protested.

"Ha, ha! Dat is funny. You tell dat to ze judge; mebbe him laugh, eh?"

"I say I did n't," he reiterated manfully. "I did n't know I 'd shipped along with a lot of thieves."

'Frisco Kid winced at this epithet, and had Joe been looking at him he would have seen a red flush mount to his face.

"And now that I do know," he continued, "I wish to be put ashore. I don't know anything about the law, but I do know something of right and wrong; and I 'm willing to take my chance with any judge for whatever wrong I have done — with all the judges in the United States, for that matter. And that 's more than you can say, Mr. Pete."

"You say dat, eh? Vaire good. But you are one big t'ief —"

"I 'm not — don't you dare call me

that again!" Joe's face was pale, and he was trembling — but not with fear.

"T'ief!" the Frenchman taunted back.

"You lie!"

Joe had not been a boy among boys for nothing. He knew the penalty which attached itself to the words he had just spoken, and he expected to receive it. So he was not overmuch surprised when he picked himself up from the floor of the cockpit an instant later, his head still ringing from a stiff blow between the eyes.

"Say dat one time more," French Pete bullied, his fist raised and prepared to strike.

Tears of anger stood in Joe's eyes, but he was calm and in deadly earnest. "When you say I am a thief, Pete, you lie. You can kill me, but still I will say you lie."

"No, you don't!" 'Frisco Kid had darted in like a cat, preventing a second blow, and shoving the Frenchman back across the cockpit.

"You leave the boy alone!" he continued, suddenly unshipping and arming himself with the heavy iron tiller, and standing between them. "This thing's gone just about as far as it's going to go. You big fool, can't you see the stuff the boy's made of? He speaks true. He's right, and he knows it, and you could kill him and he would n't give in. There's my hand on it, Joe." He turned and extended his hand to Joe, who returned the grip. "You've got spunk and you're not afraid to show it."

French Pete's mouth twisted itself in a sickly smile, but the evil gleam in his eyes gave it the lie. He shrugged his shoulders and said, "Ah! So? He does not dee-sire dat I call him pet names. Ha, ha! It is only ze sailorman play. Let us — what you call — forgive and forget, eh? Vaire good; forgive and forget."

He reached out his hand, but Joe refused to take it. 'Frisco Kid nodded approval, while French Pete, still shrug-

ging his shoulders and smiling, passed
into the cabin.

"Slack off ze main-sheet," he called
out, "and run down for Hunter's Point.
For one time I will cook ze dinner, and
den you will say dat it is ze vaire good
dinner. Ah! French Pete is ze great
cook!"

"That's the way he always does—
gets real good and cooks when he wants
to make up," 'Frisco Kid hazarded, slip-
ping the tiller into the rudder-head and
obeying the order. "But even then you
can't trust him."

Joe nodded his head, but did not speak.
He was in no mood for conversation.
He was still trembling from the excitement of the last few moments, while
deep down he questioned himself on how
he had behaved, and found nothing to be
ashamed of.

CHAPTER XIII

BEFRIENDING EACH OTHER

THE afternoon sea-breeze had sprung up and was now rioting in from the Pacific. Angel Island was fast dropping astern, and the water-front of San Francisco showing up, as the *Dazzler* plowed along before it. Soon they were in the midst of the shipping, passing in and out among the vessels which had come from the ends of the earth. Later they crossed the fairway, where the ferry steamers, crowded with passengers, passed to and fro between San Francisco and Oakland. One came so close that the passengers crowded to the side to see the gallant little sloop and the two boys in the cockpit. Joe gazed enviously at the row of down-turned faces. They were all going to their homes, while he — he was going he knew not whither, at the will of French Pete. He was half tempted to cry out for help; but the foolishness of such an act struck him, and he held his tongue. Turning his head, his eyes wandered along the smoky heights of the city, and he fell to musing on the strange way of men and ships on the sea.

'Frisco Kid watched him from the corner of his eye, following his thoughts as accurately as though he spoke them aloud.

" Got a home over there somewheres? " he queried suddenly, waving his hand in the direction of the city.

Joe started, so correctly had his thought been guessed. " Yes," he said simply.

" Tell us about it."

Joe rapidly described his home, though forced to go into greater detail because

146

of the curious questions of his companion. 'Frisco Kid was interested in everything, especially in Mrs. Bronson and Bessie. Of the latter he could not seem to tire, and poured forth question after question concerning her. So peculiar and artless were some of them that Joe could hardly forbear to smile.

"Now tell me about yours," he said when he at last had finished.

'Frisco Kid seemed suddenly to harden, and his face took on a stern look which the other had never seen there before. He swung his foot idly to and fro, and lifted a dull eye aloft to the main-peak blocks, with which, by the way, there was nothing the matter.

"Go ahead," the other encouraged.

"I have n't no home."

The four words left his mouth as though they had been forcibly ejected, and his lips came together after them almost with a snap.

Joe saw he had touched a tender spot,

147

and strove to ease the way out of it again. "Then the home you did have." He did not dream that there were lads in the world who never had known homes, or that he had only succeeded in probing deeper.

"Never had none."

"Oh!" His interest was aroused, and he now threw solicitude to the winds. "Any sisters?"

"Nope."

"Mother?"

"I was so young when she died that I don't remember her."

"Father?"

"I never saw much of him. He went to sea — anyhow, he disappeared."

"Oh!" Joe did not know what to say, and an oppressive silence, broken only by the churn of the *Dazzler's* forefoot, fell upon them.

Just then Pete came out to relieve at the tiller while they went in to eat. Both lads hailed his advent with feelings of relief, and the awkwardness vanished over the dinner, which was all their skipper had claimed it to be. Afterward 'Frisco Kid relieved Pete, and while he was eating Joe washed up the dishes and put the cabin shipshape. Then they all gathered in the stern, where the captain strove to increase the general cordiality by entertaining them with descriptions of life among the pearl-divers of the South Seas.

In this fashion the afternoon wore away. They had long since left San Francisco behind, rounded Hunter's Point, and were now skirting the San Mateo shore. Joe caught a glimpse, once, of a party of cyclists rounding a cliff on the San Bruno Road, and remembered the time when he had gone over the same ground on his own wheel. It was only a month or two before, but it seemed an age to him now, so much had there been to come between.

By the time supper had been eaten and

the things cleared away, they were well down the bay, off the marshes behind which Redwood City clustered. The wind had gone down with the sun, and the *Dazzler* was making but little headway, when they sighted a sloop bearing down upon them on the dying wind. 'Frisco Kid instantly named it as the *Reindeer*, to which French Pete, after a deep scrutiny, agreed. He seemed very much pleased at the meeting.

"Red Nelson runs her," 'Frisco Kid informed Joe. "And he's a terror and no mistake. I'm always afraid of him when he comes near. They've got something big down here, and they're always after French Pete to tackle it with them. He knows more about it, whatever it is."

Joe nodded, and looked at the approaching craft curiously. Though somewhat larger, it was built on about the same lines as the *Dazzler* — which meant, above everything else, that it was built for speed. The mainsail was so large

that it was more like that of a racing-
yacht, and it carried the points for no
less than three reefs in case of rough
weather. Aloft and on deck everything
was in place — nothing was untidy or use-
less. From running-gear to standing
rigging, everything bore evidence of thor-
ough order and smart seamanship.

The *Reindeer* came up slowly in the
gathering twilight and went to anchor a
biscuit-toss away. French Pete followed
suit with the *Dazzler*, and then went in
the skiff to pay them a visit. The two
lads stretched themselves out on top the
cabin and awaited his return.

"Do you like the life?" Joe broke
silence.

The other turned on his elbow. "Well
— I do, and then again I don't. The fresh
air, and the salt water, and all that, and
the freedom — that's all right; but I don't
like the — the —" He paused a moment,
as though his tongue had failed in its
duty, and then blurted out: "the stealing."

"Then why don't you quit it?" Joe liked the lad more than he dared confess to himself, and he felt a sudden missionary zeal come upon him.

"I will just as soon as I can turn my hand to something else."

"But why not now?"

Now is the accepted time was ringing in Joe's ears, and if the other wished to leave, it seemed a pity that he did not, and at once.

"Where can I go? What can I do? There's nobody in all the world to lend me a hand, just as there never has been. I tried it once, and learned my lesson too well to do it again in a hurry."

"Well, when I get out of this I'm going home. Guess my father was right, after all. And I don't see, maybe — what's the matter with you going with me?" He said this last without thinking, impulsively, and 'Frisco Kid knew it.

"You don't know what you're talking about," he answered. "Fancy me going

154

off with you! What 'd your father say? and—and the rest? How would he think of me? And what 'd he do?"

Joe felt sick at heart. He realized that in the spirit of the moment he had given an invitation which, on sober thought, he knew would be impossible to carry out. He tried to imagine his father receiving in his own house a stranger like 'Frisco Kid—no, that was not to be thought of. Then, forgetting his own plight, he fell to racking his brains for some other method by which 'Frisco Kid could get away from his present surroundings.

"He might turn me over to the police," the other went on, "and send me to a refuge. I 'd die first, before I 'd let that happen to me. And besides, Joe, I 'm not of your kind, and you know it. Why, I 'd be like a fish out of water, what with all the things I did n't know. Nope; I guess I 'll have to wait a little before I strike out. But there 's only one thing for you to do, and that 's to go straight home. First chance I get I 'll land you, and then I 'll deal with French Pete —"

"No, you don't," Joe interrupted hotly. "When I leave I 'm not going to leave you in trouble on my account. So don't you try anything like that. I 'll get away, never fear, and if I can figure it out I want you to come along too; come along anyway, and figure it out afterward. What d' you say?"

'Frisco Kid shook his head, and, gazing up at the starlit heavens, wandered off into dreams of the life he would like to lead but from which he seemed inexorably shut out. The seriousness of life was striking deeper than ever into Joe's heart, and he lay silent, thinking hard. A mumble of heavy voices came to them from the *Reindeer;* and from the land the solemn notes of a church bell floated across the water, while the summer night wrapped them slowly in its warm darkness.

CHAPTER XIV

AMONG THE OYSTER-BEDS

TIME and the world slipped away, and both boys were aroused by the harsh voice of French Pete from the sleep into which they had fallen.

"Get under way!" he was bawling. "Here, you Sho! Cast off ze gaskets! Queeck! Lively! You Kid, ze jib!"

Joe was clumsy in the darkness, not knowing the names of things and the places where they were to be found; but he made fair progress, and when he had tossed the gaskets into the cockpit was ordered forward to help hoist the mainsail. After that the anchor was hove in and the jib set. Then they coiled down the halyards and put everything in order before they returned aft.

"Vaire good, vaire good," the Frenchman praised, as Joe dropped in over the rail. "Splendeed! You make ze good sailorman, I know for sure."

'Frisco Kid lifted the cover of one of the cockpit lockers and glanced questioningly at French Pete.

"For sure," that mariner replied. "Put up ze side-lights."

'Frisco Kid took the red and green lanterns into the cabin to light them, and then went forward with Joe to hang them in the rigging.

"They 're not goin' to tackle it," 'Frisco Kid said in an undertone.

"What?" Joe asked.

"That big thing I was tellin' you was down here somewhere. It 's so big, I guess, that French Pete 's 'most afraid to go in for it. Red Nelson 'd go in quicker 'n a wink, but he don't know enough about it. Can't go in, you see, till Pete gives the word."

"Where are we going now?" Joe questioned.

"Don't know; oyster-beds most likely, from the way we 're heading."

It was an uneventful trip. A breeze sprang up out of the night behind them, and held steady for an hour or more. Then it dropped and became aimless and erratic, puffing gently first from one quarter and then another. French Pete remained at the tiller, while occasionally Joe or 'Frisco Kid took in or slacked off a sheet.

Joe sat and marveled that the Frenchman should know where he was going. To Joe it seemed that they were lost in the impenetrable darkness which shrouded them. A high fog had rolled in from the Pacific, and though they were beneath, it came between them and the stars, depriving them of the little light from that source.

But French Pete seemed to know instinctively the direction he should go, and once, in reply to a query from Joe, bragged of his ability to go by the "feel" of things.

"I feel ze tide, ze wind, ze speed," he explained. "Even do I feel ze land. Dat I tell you for sure. How? I do not know. Only do I know dat I feel ze land, just like my arm grow long, miles and miles long, and I put my hand upon ze land and feel it, and know dat it is there."

Joe looked incredulously at 'Frisco Kid.

"That's right," he affirmed. "After you've been on the water a good while you come to feel the land. And if your nose is any account, you can usually smell it."

An hour or so later, Joe surmised from the Frenchman's actions that they were approaching their destination. He seemed on the alert, and was constantly peering into the darkness ahead as though he expected to see something at any moment. Joe looked very hard, but saw only the darkness.

"Try ze stick, Kid," French Pete ordered. "I t'ink it is about ze time."

'Frisco Kid unlashed a long and slender pole from the top of the cabin, and, standing on the narrow deck amidships, plunged one end of it into the water and drove it straight down.

"About fifteen feet," he said.

"What ze bottom?"

"Mud," was the answer.

"Wait one while, den we try some more."

Five minutes afterward the pole was plunged overside again.

"Two fathoms," Joe answered— "shells."

French Pete rubbed his hands with satisfaction. "Vaire good, vaire well," he said. "I hit ze ground every time. You can't fool-a ze old man; I tell you dat for sure."

'Frisco Kid continued operating the pole and announcing the results, to the mystification of Joe, who could not comprehend their intimate knowledge of the bottom of the bay.

"Ten feet — shells," 'Frisco Kid went on in a monotonous voice. "'Leven feet — shells. Fourteen feet — soft. Sixteen feet — mud. No bottom."

"Ah, ze channel," said French Pete at this.

For a few minutes it was "No bottom"; and then, suddenly, came 'Frisco Kid's cry: "Eight feet — hard!"

"Dat 'll do," French Pete commanded. "Run for'ard, you Sho, an' let go ze jib. You, Kid, get all ready ze hook."

Joe found the jib-halyard and cast it off the pin, and, as the canvas fluttered down, came in hand over hand on the downhaul.

"Let 'er go!" came the command, and the anchor dropped into the water, carrying but little chain after it.

'Frisco Kid threw over plenty of slack and made fast. Then they furled the sails, made things tidy, and went below and to bed.

It was six o'clock when Joe awoke and

went out into the cockpit to look about. Wind and sea had sprung up, and the *Dazzler* was rolling and tossing and now and again fetching up on her anchor-chain with a savage jerk. He was forced to hold on to the boom overhead to steady himself. It was a gray and leaden day, with no signs of the rising sun, while the sky was obscured by great masses of flying clouds.

Joe sought for the land. A mile and a half away it lay — a long, low stretch of sandy beach with a heavy surf thundering upon it. Behind appeared desolate marsh-lands, while far beyond towered the Contra Costa Hills.

Changing the direction of his gaze, Joe was startled by the sight of a small sloop rolling and plunging at her anchor not a hundred yards away. She was nearly to windward, and as she swung off slightly he read her name on the stern, the *Flying Dutchman*, one of the boats he had seen lying at the city wharf in Oakland. A

little to the left of her he discovered the
Ghost, and beyond were half a dozen
other sloops at anchor.

"What I tell you?"

Joe looked quickly over his shoulder.
French Pete had come out of the cabin
and was triumphantly regarding the spectacle.

"What I tell you? Can't fool-a ze old
man, dat 's what. I hit it in ze dark just
so well as in ze sunshine. I know — I
know."

"Is she goin' to howl?" 'Frisco Kid
asked from the cabin, where he was starting the fire.

The Frenchman gravely studied sea
and sky for a couple of minutes.

"Mebbe blow over — mebbe blow
up," was his doubtful verdict. "Get
breakfast queeck, and we try ze dredging."

Smoke was rising from the cabins of
the different sloops, denoting that they
were all bent on getting the first meal of

the day. So far as the *Dazzler* was concerned, it was a simple matter, and soon they were putting a single reef in the mainsail and getting ready to weigh anchor.

Joe was curious. These were undoubtedly the oyster-beds; but how under the sun, in that wild sea, were they to get oysters? He was quickly to learn the way. Lifting a section of the cockpit flooring, French Pete brought out two triangular frames of steel. At the apex of one of these triangles, in a ring for the purpose, he made fast a piece of stout rope. From this the sides (inch rods) diverged at almost right angles, and extended down for a distance of four feet or more, where they were connected by the third side of the triangle, which was the bottom of the dredge. This was a flat plate of steel over a yard in length, to which was bolted a row of long, sharp teeth, likewise of steel. Attached to the toothed plate, and to the sides of the frame was a net of very coarse fishing-twine, which Joe correctly surmised was there to catch the oysters raked loose by the teeth from the bottom of the bay.

A rope being made fast to each of the dredges, they were dropped overboard from either side of the *Dazzler*. When they had reached the bottom, and were dragging with the proper length of line out, they checked her speed quite noticeably. Joe touched one of the lines with his hands, and could feel plainly the shock and jar and grind as it tore over the bottom.

"All in!" French Pete shouted.

The boys laid hold of the line and hove in the dredge. The net was full of mud and slime and small oysters, with here and there a large one. This mess they dumped on the deck and picked over while the dredge was dragging again. The large oysters they threw into the cockpit, and shoveled the rubbish overboard. There was no rest, for by this time the other dredge required emptying. And when this was done and the oysters sorted, both dredges had to be hauled aboard, so that French Pete could put the *Dazzler* about on the other tack.

The rest of the fleet was under way and dredging back in similar fashion. Sometimes the different sloops came quite close to them, and they hailed them and exchanged snatches of conversation and rough jokes. But in the main it was hard work, and at the end of an hour Joe's back was aching from the unaccustomed strain, and his fingers were cut and bleeding from his clumsy handling of the sharp-edged oysters.

"Dat 's right," French Pete said approvingly. "You learn queeck. Vaire soon you know how."

Joe grinned ruefully and wished it was dinner-time. Now and then, when a light dredge was hauled, the boys managed to catch breath and say a couple of words.

"That 's Asparagus Island," 'Frisco

Kid said, indicating the shore. "At least, that's what the fishermen and scow-sailors call it. The people who live there call it Bay Farm Island." He pointed more to the right. "And over there is San Leandro. You can't see it, but it's there."

"Ever been there?" Joe asked.

'Frisco Kid nodded his head and signed to him to help heave in the starboard dredge.

"These are what they call the deserted beds," he said again. "Nobody owns them, so the oyster pirates come down and make a bluff at working them."

"Why a bluff?"

"'Cause they're pirates, that's why, and because there's more money in raiding the private beds."

He made a sweeping gesture toward the east and southeast. "The private beds are over yonder, and if it don't storm the whole fleet 'll be raidin' 'em to-night."

"And if it does storm?" Joe asked.

"Why, we won't raid them, and French Pete 'll be mad, that 's all. He always hates being put out by the weather. But it don't look like lettin' up, and this is the worst possible shore in a sou'wester. Pete may try to hang on, but it 's best to get out before she howls."

At first it did seem as though the weather were growing better. The stiff southwest wind dropped perceptibly, and by noon, when they went to anchor for dinner, the sun was breaking fitfully through the clouds.

"That 's all right," 'Frisco Kid said prophetically. "But I ain't been on the bay for nothing. She 's just gettin' ready to let us have it good an' hard."

"I t'ink you 're right, Kid," French Pete agreed; "but ze *Dazzler* hang on all ze same. Last-a time she run away, an' fine night come. Dis time she run not away. Eh? Vaire good."

CHAPTER XV

ALL afternoon the *Dazzler* pitched and rolled at her anchorage, and as evening drew on the wind deceitfully eased down. This, and the example set by French Pete, encouraged the rest of the oyster-boats to attempt to ride out the night; but they looked carefully to their moorings and put out spare anchors.

French Pete ordered the two boys into the skiff, and, at the imminent risk of swamping, they carried out a second anchor, at nearly right angles to the first one, and dropped it over. French Pete then ran out a great quantity of chain and rope, so that the *Dazzler* dropped back a hundred feet or more, where she rode more easily.

170

Good Sailors in a Wild Anchorage

It was a wild stretch of water which Joe looked upon from the shelter of the cockpit. The oyster-beds were out in the open bay, utterly unprotected, and the wind, sweeping the water for a clean twelve miles, kicked up so tremendous a sea that at every moment it seemed as though the wallowing sloops would roll their masts overside. Just before twilight a patch of sail sprang up to windward, and grew and grew until it resolved itself into the huge mainsail of the *Reindeer*.

"Ze beeg fool!" French Pete cried, running out of the cabin to see. "Sometime—ah, sometime, I tell you—he crack on like dat, an' he go, pouf! just like dat, pouf!—an' no more Nelson, no more *Reindeer*, no more nothing."

Joe looked inquiringly at 'Frisco Kid.

"That 's right," he answered. "Nelson ought to have at least one reef in. Two 'd be better. But there he goes, every inch spread, as though some fiend was after 'im. He drives too hard; he's too reckless, when there ain't the smallest need for it. I've sailed with him, and I know his ways."

Like some huge bird of the air, the *Reindeer* lifted and soared down on them on the foaming crest of a wave.

"Don't mind," 'Frisco Kid warned. "He's only tryin' to see how close he can come to us without hittin' us."

Joe nodded, and stared with wide eyes at the thrilling sight. The *Reindeer* leaped up in the air, pointing her nose to the sky till they could see her whole churning forefoot; then she plunged downward till her for'ard deck was flush with the foam, and with a dizzying rush she drove past them, her main-boom missing the *Dazzler's* rigging by scarcely a foot.

Nelson, at the wheel, waved his hand to them as he hurtled past, and laughed joyously in French Pete's face, who was angered by the dangerous trick.

When to leeward, the splendid craft

rounded to the wind, rolling once till her brown bottom showed to the centerboard and they thought she was over, then righting and dashing ahead again like a thing possessed. She passed abreast of them on the starboard side. They saw the jib run down with a rush and an anchor go overboard as she shot into the wind; and as she fell off and back and off and back with a spilling mainsail, they saw a second anchor go overboard, wide apart from the first. Then the mainsail came down on the run, and was furled and fastened by the time she had tightened to her double hawsers.

"Ah, ah! Never was there such a man!"

The Frenchman's eyes were glistening with admiration for such perfect seamanship, and 'Frisco Kid's were likewise moist.

"Just like a yacht," he said as he went back into the cabin. "Just like a yacht, only better."

As night came on the wind began to rise again, and by eleven o'clock had reached the stage which 'Frisco Kid described as "howlin'." There was little sleep on the *Dazzler*. He alone closed his eyes. French Pete was up and down every few minutes. Twice, when he went on deck, he paid out more chain and rope. Joe lay in his blankets and listened, the while vainly courting sleep. He was not frightened, but he was untrained in the art of sleeping in the midst of such turmoil and uproar and violent commotion. Nor had he imagined a boat could play as wild antics as did the *Dazzler* and still survive. Often she wallowed over on her beam till he thought she would surely capsize. At other times she leaped and plunged in the air and fell upon the seas with thunderous crashes as though her bottom were shattered to fragments. Again, she would fetch up taut on her hawsers so suddenly and so fiercely as to reel from the shock and to groan and protest through every timber.

'Frisco Kid awoke once, and smiled at him, saying:

"This is what they call hangin' on. But just you wait till daylight comes, and watch us clawin' off. If some of the sloops don't go ashore, I 'm not me, that 's all."

And thereat he rolled over on his side and was off to sleep. Joe envied him. About three in the morning he heard French Pete crawl up for'ard and rummage around in the eyes of the boat. Joe looked on curiously, and by the dim light of the wildly swinging sea-lamp saw him drag out two spare coils of line. These he took up on deck, and Joe knew he was bending them on to the hawsers to make them still longer.

At half-past four French Pete had the fire going, and at five he called the boys for coffee. This over, they crept into the cockpit to gaze on the terrible scene. The dawn was breaking bleak and gray over a wild waste of tumbling water. They could faintly see the beach-line of

Asparagus Island, but they could distinctly hear the thunder of the surf upon it; and as the day grew stronger they made out that they had dragged fully half a mile during the night.

The rest of the fleet had likewise dragged. The *Reindeer* was almost abreast of them; *La Caprice* lay a few hundred yards away; and to leeward, straggling between them and shore, were five more of the struggling oyster-boats.

"Two missing," 'Frisco Kid announced, putting the glasses to his eyes and searching the beach.

"And there 's one!" he cried. And after studying it carefully he added: "The *Go Ask Her*. She 'll be in pieces in no time. I hope they got ashore."

French Pete looked through the glasses, and then Joe. He could clearly see the unfortunate sloop lifting and pounding in the surf, and on the beach he spied the men who made up her crew.

"Where 's ze *Ghost?*" French Pete queried.

'Frisco Kid looked for her in vain along the beach; but when he turned the glass seaward he quickly discovered her riding safely in the growing light, half a mile or more to windward.

"I 'll bet she did n't drag a hundred feet all night," he said. "Must 've struck good holding-ground."

"Mud," was French Pete's verdict. "Just one vaire small patch of mud right there. If she get t'rough it she 's a sure-enough goner, I tell you dat. Her anchors vaire light, only good for mud. I tell ze boys get more heavy anchors, but dey laugh. Some day be sorry, for sure."

One of the sloops to leeward raised a patch of sail and began the terrible struggle out of the jaws of destruction and death. They watched her for a space, rolling and plunging fearfully, and making very little headway.

French Pete put a stop to their gazing. "Come on!" he shouted. "Put two reef in ze mainsail! We get out queeck!"

While occupied with this a shout aroused them. Looking up, they saw the *Ghost* dead ahead and right on top of them, and dragging down upon them at a furious rate.

French Pete scrambled forward like a cat, at the same time drawing his knife, with one stroke of which he severed the rope that held them to the spare anchor. This threw the whole weight of the *Dazzler* on the chain-anchor. In consequence she swung off to the left, and just in time; for the next instant, drifting stern foremost, the *Ghost* passed over the spot she had vacated.

"Why, she 's got four anchors out!" Joe exclaimed, at sight of four taut ropes entering the water almost horizontally from her bow.

"Two of 'em 's dredges," 'Frisco Kid grinned; "and there goes the stove."

178

Good Sailors in a Wild Anchorage

As he spoke, two young fellows appeared on deck and dropped the cooking-stove overside with a line attached.

"Phew!" 'Frisco Kid cried. "Look at Nelson. He's got one reef in, and you can just bet that's a sign she's howlin'!"

The *Reindeer* came foaming toward them, breasting the storm like some magnificent sea-animal. Red Nelson waved to them as he passed astern, and fifteen minutes later, when they were breaking out the one anchor that remained to them, he passed well to windward on the other tack.

French Pete followed her admiringly, though he said ominously: "Some day, pouf! he go just like dat, I tell you, sure."

A moment later the *Dazzler's* reefed jib was flung out, and she was straining and struggling in the thick of the fight. It was slow work, and hard and dangerous, clawing off that lee shore, and Joe found himself marveling often that so small a craft could possibly endure a minute in such elemental fury. But little by little she worked off the shore and out of the ground-swell into the deeper waters of the bay, where the main-sheet was slacked away a bit, and she ran for shelter behind the rock wall of the Alameda Mole a few miles away. Here they found the *Reindeer* calmly at anchor; and here, during the next several hours, straggled in the remainder of the fleet, with the exception of the *Ghost*, which had evidently gone ashore to keep the *Go Ask Her* company.

By afternoon the wind had dropped away with surprising suddenness, and the weather had turned almost summer-like.

"It does n't look right," 'Frisco Kid said in the evening, after French Pete had rowed over in the skiff to visit Nelson.

"What does n't look right?" Joe asked.

"Why, the weather. It went down too sudden. It did n't have a chance to blow itself out, and it ain't going to quit till it does blow itself out. It 's likely to puff up and howl at any moment, if I know anything about it."

"Where will we go from here?" Joe asked. "Back to the oyster-beds?"

'Frisco Kid shook his head. "I can't say what French Pete 'll do. He's been fooled on the iron, and fooled on the oysters, and he's that disgusted he's liable to do 'most anything desperate. I would n't be surprised to see him go off with Nelson towards Redwood City, where that big thing is that I was tellin' you about. It's somewhere over there."

"Well, I won't have anything to do with it," Joe announced decisively.

"Of course not," 'Frisco Kid answered. "And with Nelson and his two men an' French Pete, I don't think there 'll be any need for you anyway."

CHAPTER XVI

'FRISCO KID'S DITTY-BOX

AFTER the conversation died away, the two lads lay upon the cabin for perhaps an hour. Then, without saying a word, 'Frisco Kid went below and struck a light. Joe could hear him fumbling about, and a little later heard his own name called softly. On going into the cabin, he saw 'Frisco Kid sitting on the edge of the bunk, a sailor's ditty-box on his knees, and in his hand a carefully folded page from a magazine.

"Does she look like this?" he asked, smoothing it out and turning it that the other might see.

It was a half-page illustration of two girls and a boy, grouped, evidently, in

an old-fashioned roomy attic, and holding a council of some sort. The girl
who was talking faced the onlooker,
while the backs of the other two were
turned.

"Who?" Joe queried, glancing in per-
plexity from the picture to 'Frisco Kid's
face.

"Your — your sister — Bessie."

The word seemed reluctant in coming
to his lips, and he expressed himself with a
certain shy reverence, as though it were
something unspeakably sacred.

Joe was nonplussed for the moment.
He could see no bearing between the two
in point, and, anyway, girls were rather
silly creatures to waste one's time over.
"He 's actually blushing," he thought,
regarding the soft glow on the other's
cheeks. He felt an irresistible desire to
laugh, and tried to smother it down.

"No, no; don't!" 'Frisco Kid cried,
snatching the paper away and putting it
back in the ditty-box with shaking fin-

gers. Then he added more slowly: "I thought — I — I kind o' thought you would understand, and — and —"

His lips trembled and his eyes glistened with unwonted moistness as he turned hastily away.

The next instant Joe was by his side on the bunk, his arm around him. Prompted by some instinctive monitor, he had done it before he thought. A week before he could not have imagined himself in such an absurd situation — his arm around a boy; but now it seemed the most natural thing in the world. He did not comprehend, but he knew, whatever it was, that it was of deep importance to his companion.

"Go ahead and tell us," he urged. "I'll understand."

"No, you won't. You can't."

"Yes, sure. Go ahead."

'Frisco Kid choked and shook his head. "I don't think I could, anyway. It's more the things I feel, and I don't know

184

how to put them in words." Joe's hand patted his shoulder reassuringly, and he went on: "Well, it 's this way. You see, I don't know much about the land, and people, and things, and I never had any brothers or sisters or playmates. All the time I did n't know it, but I was lonely — sort of missed them down in here somewheres." He placed a hand over his breast. "Did you ever feel downright hungry? Well, that 's just the way I used to feel, only a different kind of hunger, and me not knowing what it was. But one day, oh, a long time back, I got a-hold of a magazine and saw a picture — that picture, with the two girls and the boy talking together. I thought it must be fine to be like them, and I got to thinking about the things they said and did, till it came to me all of a sudden like, and I knew it was just loneliness was the matter with me.

"But, more than anything else, I got to wondering about the girl who looks out of the picture right at you. I was thinking about her all the time, and by and by she became real to me. You see, it was making believe, and I knew it all the time, and then again I did n't. Whenever I 'd think of the men, and the work, and the hard life, I 'd know it was make-believe; but when I 'd think of her, it was n't. I don't know; I can't explain it."

Joe remembered all his own adventures which he had imagined on land and sea, and nodded. He at least understood that much.

"Of course it was all foolishness, but to have a girl like that for a comrade or friend seemed more like heaven to me than anything else I knew of. As I said, it was a long while back, and I was only a little kid — that was when Red Nelson gave me my name, and I 've never been anything but 'Frisco Kid ever since. But the girl in the picture: I was always getting that picture out to look at her, and

188

before long, if I was n't square — why, I felt ashamed to look at her. Afterwards, when I was older, I came to look at it in another way. I thought, 'Suppose, Kid, some day you were to meet a girl like that, what would she think of you? Could she like you? Could she be even the least bit of a friend to you?' And then I 'd make up my mind to be better, to try and do something with myself so that she or any of her kind of people would not be ashamed to know me.

"That 's why I learned to read. That 's why I ran away. Nicky Perrata, a Greek boy, taught me my letters, and it was n't till after I learned to read that I found out there was anything really wrong in bay-pirating. I 'd been used to it ever since I could remember, and almost all the people I knew made their living that way. But when I did find out, I ran away, thinking to quit it for good. I 'll tell you about it sometime, and how I 'm back at it again.

"Of course she seemed a real girl when I was a youngster, and even now she sometimes seems that way, I 've thought so much about her. But while I 'm talking to you it all clears up and she comes to me in this light: she stands just for a plain idea, a better, cleaner life than this, and one I 'd like to live; and if I could live it, why, I 'd come to know that kind of girls, and their kind of people — your kind, that 's what I mean. So I was wondering about your sister and you, and that 's why — I don't know; I guess I was just wondering. But I suppose you know lots of girls like that, don't you?"

Joe nodded his head.

"Then tell me about them — something, anything," he added as he noted the fleeting expression of doubt in the other's eyes.

"Oh, that 's easy," Joe began valiantly. To a certain extent he did understand the lad's hunger, and it seemed a simple enough task to at least partially satisfy

him. "To begin with, they 're like—
hem!—why, they 're like—girls, just
girls." He broke off with a miserable
sense of failure.

'Frisco Kid waited patiently, his face a
study in expectancy.

Joe struggled valiantly to marshal his
forces. To his mind, in quick succession,
came the girls with whom he had gone to
school—the sisters of the boys he knew,
and those who were his sister's friends:
slim girls and plump girls, tall girls and
short girls, blue-eyed and brown-eyed,
curly-haired, black-haired, golden-haired;
in short, a procession of girls of all sorts
and descriptions. But, to save himself,
he could say nothing about them. Anyway, he 'd never been a "sissy," and why
should he be expected to know anything
about them? "All girls are alike," he
concluded desperately. "They 're just
the same as the ones you know, Kid—sure
they are."

"But I don't know any."

Joe whistled. "And never did?"

"Yes, one. Carlotta Gispardi. But she could n't speak English, and I could n't speak Dago; and she died. I don't care; though I never knew any, I seem to know as much about them as you do."

"And I guess I know more about adventures all over the world than you do," Joe retorted.

Both boys laughed. But a moment later, Joe fell into deep thought. It had come upon him quite swiftly that he had not been duly grateful for the good things of life he did possess. Already home, father, and mother had assumed a greater significance to him; but he now found himself placing a higher personal value upon his sister and his chums and friends. He had never appreciated them properly, he thought, but henceforth — well, there would be a different tale to tell.

The voice of French Pete hailing them put a finish to the conversation, for they both ran on deck.

CHAPTER XVII

'FRISCO KID TELLS HIS STORY

"GET up ze mainsail and break out ze hook!" the Frenchman shouted. "And den tail on to ze *Reindeer!* No side-lights!"

"Come! Cast off those gaskets — lively!" 'Frisco Kid ordered. "Now lay on to the peak-halyards—there, that rope — cast it off the pin. And don't hoist ahead of me. There! Make fast! We'll stretch it afterwards. Run aft and come in on the main-sheet! Shove the helm up!"

Under the sudden driving power of the mainsail, the *Dazzler* strained and tugged at her anchor like an impatient horse till the muddy iron left the bottom with a rush and she was free.

"Let go the sheet! Come for'ard again and lend a hand on the chain! Stand by to give her the jib!" 'Frisco Kid the boy who mooned over girls in pictorial magazines had vanished, and 'Frisco Kid the sailor, strong and dominant, was on deck. He ran aft and tacked about as the jib rattled aloft in the hands of Joe, who quickly joined him. Just then the *Reindeer*, like a monstrous bat, passed to leeward of them in the gloom.

"Ah, dose boys! Dey take all-a night!" they heard French Pete exclaim, and then the gruff voice of Red Nelson, who said: "Never you mind, Frenchy. I taught the Kid his sailorizing, and I ain't never been ashamed of him yet."

The *Reindeer* was the faster boat, but by spilling the wind from her sails they managed so that the boys could keep them in sight. The breeze came steadily in from the west, with a promise of early increase. The stars were being blotted out by masses of driving clouds, which indicated a greater velocity in the upper strata. 'Frisco Kid surveyed the sky.

" Going to have it good and stiff before morning," he said, " just as I told you."

Several hours later, both boats stood in for the San Mateo shore, and dropped anchor not more than a cable's-length away. A little wharf ran out, the bare end of which was perceptible to them, though they could discern a small yacht lying moored to a buoy a short distance away.

According to their custom, everything was put in readiness for hasty departure. The anchors could be tripped and the sails flung out on a moment's notice. Both skiffs came over noiselessly from the *Reindeer*. Red Nelson had given one of his two men to French Pete, so that each skiff was doubly manned. They were not a very prepossessing group of men,—at least, Joe did not think so,—for their faces bore a savage seriousness which almost made him shiver. The captain of the *Dazzler* buckled on his pistol-belt, and placed a rifle and a stout double-block tackle in the boat. Then he poured out wine all around, and, standing in the darkness of the little cabin, they pledged success to the expedition. Red Nelson was also armed, while his men wore at their hips the customary sailor's sheath-knife. They were very slow and careful to avoid noise in getting into the boats, French Pete pausing long enough to warn the boys to remain quietly aboard and not try any tricks.

"Now 'd be your chance, Joe, if they had n't taken the skiff," 'Frisco Kid whispered, when the boats had vanished into the loom of the land.

"What 's the matter with the *Dazzler?*" was the unexpected answer. "We could up sail and away before you could say Jack Robinson."

'Frisco Kid hesitated. The spirit of comradeship was strong in the lad, and deserting a companion in a pinch could not but be repulsive to him.

"I don't think it 'd be exactly square to leave them in the lurch ashore," he said. "Of course," he went on hurriedly, "I know the whole thing 's wrong; but you remember that first night, when you came running through the water for the skiff, and those fellows on the bank busy popping away? We did n't leave you in the lurch, did we?"

Joe assented reluctantly, and then a new thought flashed across his mind. "But they 're pirates — and thieves — and criminals. They 're breaking the law, and you and I are not willing to be law-breakers. Besides, they 'll not be left. There 's the *Reindeer*. There 's nothing to prevent them from getting away on her, and they 'll never catch us in the dark."

"Come on, then." Though he had agreed, 'Frisco Kid did not quite like it, for it still seemed to savor of desertion.

They crawled forward and began to hoist the mainsail. The anchor they could slip, if necessary, and save the time of pulling it up. But at the first rattle

197

of the halyards on the sheaves a warning "Hist!" came to them through the darkness, followed by a loudly whispered "Drop that!"

Glancing in the direction from which these sounds proceeded, they made out a white face peering at them from over the rail of the other sloop.

"Aw, it's only the *Reindeer's* boy," 'Frisco Kid said. "Come on."

Again they were interrupted at the first rattling of the blocks.

"I say, you fellers, you'd better let go them halyards pretty quick, I'm a-tellin' you, or I'll give you what for!"

This threat being dramatically capped by the click of a cocking pistol, 'Frisco Kid obeyed and went grumblingly back to the cockpit. "Oh, there's plenty more chances to come," he whispered consolingly to Joe. "French Pete was cute, wasn't he? He thought you might be trying to make a break, and put a guard on us."

Nothing came from the shore to indicate how the pirates were faring. Not a dog barked, not a light flared. Yet the air seemed quivering with an alarm about to burst forth. The night had taken on a strained feeling of intensity, as though it held in store all kinds of terrible things. The boys felt this keenly as they huddled against each other in the cockpit and waited.

"You were going to tell me about your running away," Joe ventured finally, "and why you came back again."

'Frisco Kid took up the tale at once, speaking in a muffled undertone close to the other's ear.

"You see, when I made up my mind to quit the life, there was n't a soul to lend me a hand; but I knew that the only thing for me to do was to get ashore and find some kind of work, so I could study. Then I figured there 'd be more chance in the country than in the city; so I gave Red Nelson the slip — I was on the

Reindeer then. One night on the Alameda oyster-beds, I got ashore and headed back from the bay as fast as I could sprint. Nelson did n't catch me. But they were all Portuguese farmers thereabouts, and none of them had work for me. Besides, it was in the wrong time of the year — winter. That shows how much I knew about the land.

"I 'd saved up a couple of dollars, and I kept traveling back, deeper and deeper into the country, looking for work, and buying bread and cheese and such things from the storekeepers. I tell you, it was cold, nights, sleeping out without blankets, and I was always glad when morning came. But worse than that was the way everybody looked on me. They were all suspicious, and not a bit afraid to show it, and sometimes they 'd set their dogs on me and tell me to get along. Seemed as though there was n't any place for me on the land. Then my money gave out, and just about the time I was good and hungry I got captured."

"Captured! What for?"

"Nothing. Living, I suppose. I crawled into a haystack to sleep one night, because it was warmer, and along comes a village constable and arrests me for being a tramp. At first they thought I was a runaway, and telegraphed my description all over. I told them I did n't have any people, but they would n't believe me for a long while. And then, when nobody claimed me, the judge sent me to a boys' 'refuge' in San Francisco."

He stopped and peered intently in the direction of the shore. The darkness and the silence in which the men had been swallowed up was profound. Nothing was stirring save the rising wind.

"I thought I 'd die in that 'refuge.' It was just like being in jail. We were locked up and guarded like prisoners. Even then, if I could have liked the other boys it might have been all right. But they were mostly street-boys of the worst kind—lying, and sneaking, and cowardly, without one spark of manhood or one idea of square dealing and fair play. There was only one thing I did like, and that was the books. Oh, I did lots of reading, I tell you! But that could n't make up for the rest. I wanted the freedom and the sunlight and the salt water. And what had I done to be kept in prison and herded with such a gang? Instead of doing wrong, I had tried to do right, to make myself better, and that 's what I got for it. I was n't old enough, you see, to reason anything out.

"Sometimes I 'd see the sunshine dancing on the water and showing white on the sails, and the *Reindeer* cutting through it just as you please, and I 'd get that sick I would know hardly what I did. And then the boys would come against me with some of their meannesses, and I 'd start in to lick the whole kit of them. Then the men in charge would lock me up and punish me. Well, I could n't stand it any longer; I watched my chance and ran for it. Seemed as though there was n't any place on the land for me, so I picked up with French Pete and went back on the bay. That 's about all there is to it, though I 'm going to try it again when I get a little older — old enough to get a square deal for myself."

"You 're going to go back on the land with me," Joe said authoritatively, laying a hand on his shoulder. "That 's what you 're going to do. As for — "

Bang! a revolver-shot rang out from the shore. Bang! bang! More guns were speaking sharply and hurriedly. A man's voice rose wildly on the air and died away. Somebody began to cry for help. Both boys were on their feet on the instant, hoisting the mainsail and getting everything ready to run. The *Reindeer* boy was doing likewise. A man, roused from his sleep on the yacht, thrust an excited head through the skylight, but withdrew it hastily at sight of the two stranger sloops. The intensity of waiting was broken, the time for action come.

CHAPTER XVIII

A NEW RESPONSIBILITY FOR JOE

HEAVING in on the anchor-chain till it was up and down, 'Frisco Kid and Joe ceased from their exertions. Everything was in readiness to give the *Dazzler* the jib, and go. They strained their eyes in the direction of the shore. The clamor had died away, but here and there lights were beginning to flash. The creaking of a block and tackle came to their ears, and they heard Red Nelson's voice singing out: "Lower away!" and "Cast off!"

"French Pete forgot to oil it," 'Frisco Kid commented, referring to the tackle.

"Takin' their time about it, ain't they?" the boy on the *Reindeer* called over to them, sitting down on the cabin and mopping his face after the exertion of hoisting the mainsail single-handed.

"Guess they 're all right," 'Frisco Kid rejoined. "All ready?"

"Yes — all right here."

"Say, you," the man on the yacht cried through the skylight, not venturing to show his head. "You 'd better go away."

"And you 'd better stay below and keep quiet," was the response. "We 'll take care of ourselves. You do the same."

"If I was only out of this, I 'd show you!" he threatened.

"Lucky for you you 're not," responded the boy on the *Reindeer;* and thereat the man kept quiet.

"Here they come!" said 'Frisco Kid suddenly to Joe.

The two skiffs shot out of the darkness and came alongside. Some kind of an altercation was going on, as French Pete's voice attested.

"No, no!" he cried. "Put it on ze

Dazzler. Ze *Reindeer* she sail too fast-a, and run away, oh, so queeck, and never more I see it. Put it on ze *Dazzler.* Eh? Wot you say?"

"All right then," Red Nelson agreed. "We'll whack up afterwards. But, say, hurry up. Out with you, lads, and heave her up! My arm's broke."

The men tumbled out, ropes were cast inboard, and all hands, with the exception of Joe, tailed on. The shouting of men, the sound of oars, and the rattling and slapping of blocks and sails, told that the men on shore were getting under way for the pursuit.

"Now!" Red Nelson commanded. "All together! Don't let her come back or you'll smash the skiff. There she takes it! A long pull and a strong pull! Once again! And yet again! Get a turn there, somebody, and take a spell."

Though the task was but half accomplished, they were exhausted by the strenuous effort, and hailed the rest ea-

They swung the safe into the "Dazzler"

gerly. Joe glanced over the side to discover what the heavy object might be, and saw the vague outlines of a small office-safe.

"Now all together!" Red Nelson began again. "Take her on the run and don't let her stop! Yo, ho! heave, ho! Once again! And another! Over with her!"

Straining and gasping, with tense muscles and heaving chests, they brought the cumbersome weight over the side, rolled it on top of the rail, and lowered it into the cockpit on the run. The cabin doors were thrown apart, and it was moved along, end for end, till it lay on the cabin floor, snug against the end of the centerboard-case. Red Nelson had followed it aboard to superintend. His left arm hung helpless at his side, and from the finger-tips blood dripped with monotonous regularity. He did not seem to mind it, however, nor even the mutterings of the human storm he had raised ashore, and which, to judge by the sounds, was even then threatening to break upon them.

"Lay your course for the Golden Gate," he said to French Pete, as he turned to go. "I 'll try to stand by you, but if you get lost in the dark I 'll meet you outside, off the Farralones, in the morning." He sprang into the skiff after the men, and, with a wave of his uninjured arm, cried heartily: "And then it 's for Mexico, my lads — Mexico and summer weather!"

Just as the *Dazzler*, freed from her anchor, paid off under the jib and filled away, a dark sail loomed under their stern, barely missing the skiff in tow. The cockpit of the stranger was crowded with men, who raised their voices angrily at sight of the pirates. Joe had half a mind to run forward and cut the halyards so that the *Dazzler* might be captured. As he had told French Pete the day before, he had done nothing to be ashamed of,

and was not afraid to go before a court
of justice. But the thought of 'Frisco
Kid restrained him. He wanted to take
him ashore with him, but in so doing he
did not wish to take him to jail. So he,
too, began to experience a keen interest
in the escape of the *Dazzler*.

The pursuing sloop rounded up hurriedly to come about after them, and in
the darkness fouled the yacht which lay
at anchor. The man aboard of her,
thinking that at last his time had come,
gave one wild yell, ran on deck, and
leaped overboard. In the confusion of
the collision, and while they were endea-
voring to save him, French Pete and the
boys slipped away into the night.

The *Reindeer* had already disappeared,
and by the time Joe and 'Frisco Kid had
the running-gear coiled down and everything in shape, they were standing out in
open water. The wind was freshening
constantly, and the *Dazzler* heeled a
lively clip through the comparatively

smooth stretch. Before an hour had passed, the lights of Hunter's Point were well on her starboard beam. 'Frisco Kid went below to make coffee, but Joe remained on deck, watching the lights of South San Francisco grow, and speculating on their destination. Mexico! They were going to sea in such a frail craft! Impossible! At least, it seemed so to him, for his conceptions of ocean travel were limited to steamers and full-rigged ships. He was beginning to feel half sorry that he had not cut the halyards, and longed to ask French Pete a thousand questions; but just as the first was on his lips that worthy ordered him to go below and get some coffee and then to turn in. He was followed shortly afterward by 'Frisco Kid, French Pete remaining at his lonely task of beating down the bay and out to sea. Twice he heard the waves buffeted back from some flying forefoot, and once he saw a sail to leeward on the opposite tack, which luffed

sharply and came about at sight of him.
But the darkness favored, and he heard
no more of it — perhaps because he
worked into the wind closer by a point,
and held on his way with a shaking
after-leech.

Shortly after dawn, the two boys were
called and came sleepily on deck. The
day had broken cold and gray, while the
wind had attained half a gale. Joe noted
with astonishment the white tents of the
quarantine station on Angel Island. San
Francisco lay a smoky blur on the south-
ern horizon, while the night, still linger-
ing on the western edge of the world,
slowly withdrew before their eyes.
French Pete was just finishing a long
reach into the Raccoon Straits, and at the
same time studiously regarding a plunging sloop-yacht half a mile astern.

"Dey t'ink to catch ze *Dazzler*, eh?
Bah!" And he brought the craft in question about, laying a course straight for
the Golden Gate.

The pursuing yacht followed suit. Joe watched her a few moments. She held an apparently parallel course to them, and forged ahead much faster.

"Why, at this rate they 'll have us in no time!" he cried.

French Pete laughed. "You t'ink so? Bah! Dey outfoot; we outpoint. Dey are scared of ze wind; we wipe ze eye of ze wind. Ah! you wait, you see."

"They 're traveling ahead faster," 'Frisco Kid explained, "but we 're sailing closer to the wind. In the end we 'll beat them, even if they have the nerve to cross the bar — which I don't think they have. Look! See!"

Ahead could be seen the great ocean surges, flinging themselves skyward and bursting into roaring caps of smother. In the midst of it, now rolling her dripping bottom clear, now sousing her deck-load of lumber far above the guards, a coasting steam-schooner was lumbering drunkenly into port. It was magnificent — this

battle between man and the elements.
Whatever timidity he had entertained
fled away, and Joe's nostrils began to
dilate and his eyes to flash at the near-
ness of the impending struggle.

French Pete called for his oilskins and
sou'wester, and Joe also was equipped
with a spare suit. Then he and 'Frisco
Kid were sent below to lash and cleat the
safe in place. In the midst of this task
Joe glanced at the firm-name, gilt-let-
tered on the face of it, and read: " Bronson & Tate." Why, that was his father
and his father's partner. That was their
safe, their money! 'Frisco Kid, nailing
the last cleat on the floor of the cabin,
looked up and followed his fascinated
gaze.

" That 's rough, is n't it," he whispered.
" Your father? "

Joe nodded. He could see it all now.
They had run into San Andreas, where
his father worked the big quarries, and
most probably the safe contained the

wages of the thousand men or more whom he employed. "Don't say anything," he cautioned.

'Frisco Kid agreed knowingly. "French Pete can't read, anyway," he muttered, "and the chances are that Red Nelson won't know what *your* name is. But, just the same, it's pretty rough. They'll break it open and divide up as soon as they can, so I don't see what you're going to do about it."

"Wait and see."

Joe had made up his mind that he would do his best to stand by his father's property. At the worst, it could only be lost; and that would surely be the case were he not along, while, being along, he at least had a fighting chance to save it, or to be in position to recover it. Responsibilities were showering upon him thick and fast. But a few days back he had had but himself to consider; then, in some subtle way, he had felt a certain accountability for 'Frisco Kid's future welfare; and after that, and still more subtly, he had become aware of duties which he owed to his position, to his sister, to his chums and friends; and now, by a most unexpected chain of circumstances, came the pressing need of service for his father's sake. It was a call upon his deepest strength, and he responded bravely. While the future might be doubtful, he had no doubt of himself; and this very state of mind, this self-confidence, by a generous alchemy, gave him added resolution. Nor did he fail to be vaguely aware of it, and to grasp dimly at the truth that confidence breeds confidence — strength, strength.

ALCATRAZ ISLAND

CHAPTER XIX

THE BOYS PLAN AN ESCAPE

"NOW she takes it!" French Pete cried.

Both lads ran into the cockpit. They were on the edge of the breaking bar. A huge forty-footer reared a foam-crested head far above them, stealing their wind for the moment and threatening to crush the tiny craft like an egg-shell. Joe held his breath. It was the supreme moment. French Pete luffed straight into it, and the *Dazzler* mounted the steep slope with a rush, poised a moment on the giddy summit, and fell into the yawning valley beyond. Keeping off in the intervals to fill the mainsail, and luffing into the combers, they worked their way across the

216

dangerous stretch. Once they caught
the tail-end of a whitecap and were well-
nigh smothered in the froth, but otherwise the sloop bobbed and ducked with
the happy facility of a cork.

To Joe it seemed as though he had
been lifted out of himself — out of the
world. Ah, this was life! this was action! Surely it could not be the old, com-
monplace world he had lived in so long!
The sailors, grouped on the streaming
deck-load of the steamer, waved their
sou'westers, and, on the bridge, even the
captain was expressing his admiration for
the plucky craft.

"Ah, you see! you see!" French Pete
pointed astern.

The sloop-yacht had been afraid to ven-
ture it, and was skirting back and forth
on the inner edge of the bar. The chase
was over. A pilot-boat, running for shelter from the coming storm, flew by them
like a frightened bird, passing the steamer
as though the latter were standing still.

The Cruise of the Dazzler

Half an hour later the *Dazzler* sped beyond the last smoking sea and was sliding up and down on the long Pacific swell. The wind had increased its velocity and necessitated a reefing down of jib and mainsail. Then they laid off again, full and free on the starboard tack, for the Farralones, thirty miles away. By the time breakfast was cooked and eaten they picked up the *Reindeer*, which was hove to and working offshore to the south and west. The wheel was lashed down, and there was not a soul on deck.

French Pete complained bitterly against such recklessness. "Dat is ze one fault of Red Nelson. He no care. He is afraid of not'ing. Some day he will die, oh, so vaire queeck! I know he will."

Three times they circled about the *Reindeer*, running under her weather quarter and shouting in chorus, before they brought anybody on deck. Sail was then made at once, and together the two cockle-shells plunged away into the vast-

220

ness of the Pacific. This was necessary, as 'Frisco Kid informed Joe, in order to have an offing before the whole fury of the storm broke upon them. Otherwise they would be driven on the lee shore of the California coast. Grub and water, he said, could be obtained by running into the land when fine weather came. He congratulated Joe upon the fact that he was not seasick, which circumstance likewise brought praise from French Pete and put him in better humor with his mutinous young sailor.

"I 'll tell you what we 'll do," 'Frisco Kid whispered, while cooking dinner. "Tonight we 'll drag French Pete down—"

"Drag French Pete down!"

"Yes, and tie him up good and snug, as soon as it gets dark; then put out the lights and make a run for land; get to port anyway, anywhere, just so long as we shake loose from Red Nelson."

"Yes," Joe deliberated; "that would be all right — if I could do it alone. But as for asking you to help me—why, that would be treason to French Pete."

"That 's what I 'm coming to. I 'll help you if you promise me a few things. French Pete took me aboard when I ran away from the 'refuge,' when I was starving and had no place to go, and I just can't repay him for that by sending him to jail. 'T would n't be square. Your father would n't have you break your word, would he?"

"No; of course not." Joe knew how sacredly his father held his word of honor.

"Then you must promise, and your father must see it carried out, not to press any charge against French Pete."

"All right. And now, what about yourself? You can't very well expect to go away with him again on the *Dazzler!*"

"Oh, don't bother about me. There 's nobody to miss me. I 'm strong enough, and know enough about it, to ship to sea as ordinary seaman. I 'll go away somewhere over on the other side of the world, and begin all over again."

" Then we 'll have to call it off, that 's all."

" Call what off ?"

" Tying French Pete up and running for it."

" No, sir. That 's decided upon."

" Now listen here: I 'll not have a thing to do with it. I 'll go on to Mexico first, if you don't make me one promise."

" And what 's the promise?"

" Just this: you place yourself in my hands from the moment we get ashore, and trust to me. You don't know anything about the land, anyway — you said so. And I 'll fix it with my father — I know I can — so that you can get to know people of the right sort, and study and get an education, and be something else than a bay pirate or a sailor. That 's what you 'd like, is n't it?"

Though he said nothing, 'Frisco Kid showed how well he liked it by the expression of his face.

" And it 'll be no more than your due,

223

either," Joe continued. "You will have
stood by me, and you 'll have recovered
my father's money. He 'll owe it to
you."

"But I don't do things that way.
I don't think much of a man who does
a favor just to be paid for it."

"Now you keep quiet. How much
do you think it would cost my father for
detectives and all that to recover that
safe? Give me your promise, that 's all,
and when I 've got things arranged, if
you don't like them you can back out.
Come on; that 's fair."

They shook hands on the bargain, and
proceeded to map out their line of action
for the night.

But the storm, yelling down out of the
northwest, had something entirely different in store for the *Dazzler* and her crew.
By the time dinner was over they were
forced to put double reefs in mainsail and

jib, and still the gale had not reached its height. The sea, also, had been kicked up till it was a continuous succession of water-mountains, frightful and withal grand to look upon from the low deck of the sloop. It was only when the sloops were tossed upon the crests of the waves at the same time that they caught sight of each other. Occasional fragments of seas swashed into the cockpit or dashed aft over the cabin, and Joe was stationed at the small pump to keep the well dry.

At three o'clock, watching his chance, French Pete motioned to the *Reindeer* that he was going to heave to and get out a sea-anchor. This latter was of the nature of a large shallow canvas bag, with the mouth held open by triangularly lashed spars. To this the towing-ropes were attached, on the kite principle, so that the greatest resisting surface was presented to the water. The sloop, drifting so much faster, would thus be held bow on to both wind and sea — the safest possible position in a storm. Red Nelson waved his hand in response that he understood and to go ahead.

French Pete went forward to launch the sea-anchor himself, leaving it to 'Frisco Kid to put the helm down at the proper moment and run into the wind. The Frenchman poised on the slippery foredeck, waiting an opportunity. But at that moment the *Dazzler* lifted into an unusually large sea, and, as she cleared the summit, caught a heavy snort of the gale at the very instant she was righting herself to an even keel. Thus there was not the slightest yield to this sudden pressure on her sails and mast-gear.

There was a quick snap, followed by a crash. The steel weather-rigging carried away at the lanyards, and mast, jib, mainsail, blocks, stays, sea-anchor, French Pete — everything — went over the side. Almost by a miracle, the captain clutched at the bobstay and managed to get one hand up and over the bowsprit. The boys ran forward to drag him into safety, and Red Nelson, observing the disaster, put up his helm and ran down to the rescue.

CHAPTER XX

FRENCH PETE was uninjured from the fall overboard with the *Dazzler's* mast; but the sea-anchor, which had gone with him, had not escaped so easily. The gaff of the mainsail had been driven through it, and it refused to work. The wreckage, thumping alongside, held the sloop in a quartering slant to the seas— not so dangerous a position as it might be, nor so safe, either.

"Good-by, old-a *Dazzler*. Never no more you wipe ze eye of ze wind. Never no more you kick your heels at ze crack gentlemen-yachts."

So the captain lamented, standing in the cockpit and surveying the ruin with

228

wet eyes. Even Joe, who bore him great dislike, felt sorry for him at this moment. A heavier blast of the wind caught the jagged crest of a wave and hurled it upon the helpless craft.

"Can't we save her?" Joe spluttered.

"'Frisco Kid shook his head.

"Nor the safe?"

"Impossible," he answered. "Could n't lay another boat alongside for a United States mint. As it is, it 'll keep us guessing to save ourselves."

Another sea swept over them, and the skiff, which had long since been swamped, dashed itself to pieces against the stern. Then the *Reindeer* towered above them on a mountain of water. Joe caught himself half shrinking back, for it seemed she would fall down squarely on top of them; but the next instant she dropped into the gaping trough, and they were looking down upon her far below. It was a striking picture — one Joe was destined never to forget. The *Reindeer* was

wallowing in the snow-white smother,
her rails flush with the sea, the water
scudding across her deck in foaming cat-
aracts. The air was filled with flying
spray, which made the scene appear hazy
and unreal. One of the men was clinging to the perilous after-deck and striving
to cast off the water-logged skiff. The
boy, leaning far over the cockpit-rail and
holding on for dear life, was passing him
a knife. The second man stood at the
wheel, putting it up with flying hands
and forcing the sloop to pay off. Beside
him, his injured arm in a sling, was Red
Nelson, his sou'wester gone and his fair
hair plastered in wet, wind-blown ring-
lets about his face. His whole attitude
breathed indomitability, courage, strength.
It seemed almost as though the divine
were blazing forth from him. Joe looked
upon him in sudden awe, and, realizing
the enormous possibilities of the man, felt
sorrow for the way in which they had been
wasted. A thief and a robber! In that

flashing moment Joe caught a glimpse
of human truth, grasped at the mystery
of success and failure. Life threw back
its curtains that he might read it and
understand. Of such stuff as Red Nelson were heroes made; but they possessed
wherein he lacked — the power of choice,
the careful poise of mind, the sober control
of soul: in short, the very things his father
had so often "preached" to him about.

These were the thoughts which came
to Joe in the flight of a second. Then
the *Reindeer* swept skyward and hurtled
across their bow to leeward on the breast
of a mighty billow.

"Ze wild man! ze wild man!" French
Pete shrieked, watching her in amaze-
ment. "He t'inks he can jibe! He will
die! We will all die! He must come
about. Oh, ze fool, ze fool!"

But time was precious, and Red Nelson ventured the chance. At the right
moment he jibed the mainsail over and
hauled back on the wind.

"Here she comes! Make ready to jump for it," 'Frisco Kid cried to Joe.

The *Reindeer* dashed by their stern, heeling over till the cabin windows were buried, and so close that it appeared she must run them down. But a freak of the waters lurched the two crafts apart. Red Nelson, seeing that the manœuver had miscarried, instantly instituted another. Throwing the helm hard up, the *Reindeer* whirled on her heel, thus swinging her overhanging main-boom closer to the *Dazzler*. French Pete was the nearest, and the opportunity could last no longer than a second. Like a cat he sprang, catching the foot-rope with both hands. Then the *Reindeer* forged ahead, dipping him into the sea at every plunge. But he clung on, working inboard every time he emerged, till he dropped into the cockpit as Red Nelson squared off to run down to leeward and repeat the manœuver.

"Your turn next," 'Frisco Kid said.

"No; yours," Joe replied.

"But I know more about the water," 'Frisco Kid insisted.

"And I can swim as well as you," the other retorted.

It would have been hard to forecast the outcome of this dispute; but, as it was, the swift rush of events made any settlement needless. The *Reindeer* had jibed over and was plowing back at breakneck speed, careening at such an angle that it seemed she must surely capsize. It was a gallant sight. Just then the storm burst in all its fury, the shouting wind flattening the ragged crests till they boiled. The *Reindeer* dipped from view behind an immense wave. The wave rolled on, but the next moment, where the sloop had been, the boys noted with startled eyes only the angry waters! Doubting, they looked a second time. There was no *Reindeer*. They were alone on the torn crest of the ocean!

"God have mercy on their souls!" 'Frisco Kid said solemnly.

Joe was too horrified at the suddenness of the catastrophe to utter a sound.

"Sailed her clean under, and, with the ballast she carried, went straight to bottom," 'Frisco Kid gasped. Then, turning to their own pressing need, he said: "Now we 've got to look out for ourselves. The back of the storm broke in that puff, but the sea 'll kick up worse yet as the wind eases down. Lend a hand and hang on with the other. We 've got to get her head-on."

Together, knives in hand, they crawled forward to where the pounding wreckage hampered the boat sorely. 'Frisco Kid took the lead in the ticklish work, but Joe obeyed orders like a veteran. Every minute or two the bow was swept by the sea, and they were pounded and buffeted about like a pair of shuttlecocks. First the main portion of the wreckage was securely fastened to the forward bitts; then, breathless and gasping, more often under the water than out, they cut and hacked

234

at the tangle of halyards, sheets, stays, and tackles. The cockpit was taking water rapidly, and it was a race between swamping and completing the task. At last, however, everything stood clear save the lee rigging. 'Frisco Kid slashed the lanyards. The storm did the rest. The *Dazzler* drifted swiftly to leeward of the wreckage till the strain on the line fast to the forward bitts jerked her bow into place and she ducked dead into the eye of the wind and sea.

Pausing only for a cheer at the success of their undertaking, the two lads raced aft, where the cockpit was half full and the dunnage of the cabin all afloat. With a couple of buckets procured from the stern lockers, they proceeded to fling the water overboard. It was heartbreaking work, for many a barrelful was flung back upon them again; but they persevered, and when night fell the *Dazzler*, bobbing merrily at her sea-anchor, could boast that her pumps sucked once more.

As 'Frisco Kid had said, the backbone of the storm was broken, though the wind had veered to the west, where it still blew stiffly.

"If she holds," 'Frisco Kid said, referring to the breeze, "we 'll drift to the California coast sometime to-morrow. Nothing to do now but wait."

They said little, oppressed by the loss of their comrades and overcome with exhaustion, preferring to huddle against each other for the sake of warmth and companionship. It was a miserable night, and they shivered constantly from the cold. Nothing dry was to be obtained aboard, food, blankets, everything being soaked with the salt water. Sometimes they dozed; but these intervals were short and harassing, for it seemed each took turn in waking with such sudden starts as to rouse the other.

At last day broke, and they looked about. Wind and sea had dropped considerably, and there was no question as to the safety of the *Dazzler*. The coast was nearer than they had expected, its cliffs showing dark and forbidding in the gray of dawn. But with the rising of the sun they could see the yellow beaches, flanked by the white surf, and beyond — it seemed too good to be true — the clustering houses and smoking chimneys of a town.

"Santa Cruz!" 'Frisco Kid cried, "and no chance of being wrecked in the surf!"

"Then the safe *is* safe?" Joe queried.

"Safe! I should say so. It ain't much of a sheltered harbor for large vessels, but with this breeze we'll run right up the mouth of the San Lorenzo River. Then there's a little lake like, and a boat-house. Water smooth as glass and hardly over your head. You see, I was down here once before, with Red Nelson. Come on. We'll be in in time for breakfast."

Bringing to light some spare coils of rope from the lockers, he put a clove-hitch on the standing part of the sea-anchor hawser, and carried the new running-line aft, making it fast to the stern bitts. Then he cast off from the forward bitts. The *Dazzler* swung off into the trough, completed the evolution, and pointed her nose toward shore. A couple of spare oars from below, and as many water-soaked blankets, sufficed to make a jury-mast and sail. When this was in place, Joe cast loose from the wreckage, which was now towing astern, while 'Frisco Kid took the tiller.

CHAPTER XXI

JOE AND HIS FATHER

"HOW 'S that ?" cried 'Frisco Kid, as he finished making the *Dazzler* fast fore and aft, and sat down on the string-piece of the tiny wharf. What 'll we do next, captain?"

Joe looked up in quick surprise. "Why — I — what 's the matter?"

"Well, ain't you captain now? Have n't we reached land? I 'm crew from now on, ain't I? What 's your orders?"

Joe caught the spirit of it. "Pipe all hands for breakfast — that is — wait a minute."

Diving below, he possessed himself of the money he had stowed away in his bundle when he came aboard. Then he

239

locked the cabin door, and they went up-town in search of a restaurant. Over the breakfast Joe planned the next move, and, when they had done, communicated it to 'Frisco Kid.

In response to his inquiry, the cashier told him when the morning train started for San Francisco. He glanced at the clock.

"Just time to catch it," he said to 'Frisco Kid. "Keep the cabin doors locked, and don't let anybody come aboard. Here's money. Eat at the restaurants. Dry your blankets and sleep in the cockpit. I'll be back to-morrow. And don't let anybody into that cabin. Good-by."

With a hasty hand-grip, he sped down the street to the depot. The conductor looked at him with surprise when he punched his ticket. And well he might, for it was not the custom of his passengers to travel in sea-boots and sou'west-ers. But Joe did not mind. He did not even notice. He had bought a paper and was absorbed in its contents. Before long his eyes caught an interesting paragraph:

SUPPOSED TO HAVE BEEN LOST

The tug *Sea Queen*, chartered by Bronson & Tate, has returned from a fruitless cruise outside the Heads. No news of value could be obtained concerning the pirates who so daringly carried off their safe at San Andreas last Tuesday night. The lighthouse-keeper at the Farralones mentions having sighted the two sloops Wednesday morning, clawing offshore in the teeth of the gale. It is supposed by shipping men that they perished in the storm with their ill-gotten treasure. Rumor has it that, in addition to the ten thousand dollars in gold, the safe contained papers of great importance.

When Joe had read this he felt a great relief. It was evident no one had been killed at San Andreas the night of the robbery, else there would have been some comment on it in the paper. Nor, if they had had any clue to his own whereabouts, would they have omitted such a striking bit of information.

At the depot in San Francisco the curious onlookers were surprised to see a boy clad conspicuously in sea-boots and sou'wester hail a cab and dash away. But Joe was in a hurry. He knew his father's hours, and was fearful lest he should not catch him before he went to lunch.

The office-boy scowled at him when he pushed open the door and asked to see Mr. Bronson; nor could the head clerk, when summoned by this disreputable intruder, recognize him.

"Don't you know me, Mr. Willis?"

Mr. Willis looked a second time. "Why, it's Joe Bronson! Of all things under the sun, where did you drop from? Go right in. Your father's in there."

Mr. Bronson stopped dictating to his stenographer and looked up. "Hello! Where have you been?" he said.

"To sea," Joe answered demurely, not sure of just what kind of a reception he was to get, and fingering his sou'wester nervously.

"Short trip, eh? How did you make out?"

"Oh, so-so." He had caught the twinkle in his father's eye and knew that it was all clear sailing. "Not so bad — er — that is, considering."

"Considering?"

"Well, not exactly that; rather, it might have been worse, while it could n't have been better."

"That's interesting. Sit down." Then, turning to the stenographer: "You may go, Mr. Brown, and — hum! — I won't need you any more to-day."

It was all Joe could do to keep from crying, so kindly and naturally had his father received him, making him feel at once as if not the slightest thing uncommon had occurred. It seemed as if he had just returned from a vacation, or, man-grown, had come back from some business trip.

"Now go ahead, Joe. You were speaking to me a moment ago in conundrums, and you have aroused my curiosity to a most uncomfortable degree."

Whereupon Joe sat down and told what had happened — all that had happened —from Monday night to that very moment. Each little incident he related,— every detail,— not forgetting his conversations with 'Frisco Kid nor his plans concerning him. His face flushed and he was carried away with the excitement of the narrative, while Mr. Bronson was almost as eager, urging him on whenever he slackened his pace, but otherwise remaining silent.

"So you see," Joe concluded, "it could n't possibly have turned out any better."

"Ah, well," Mr. Bronson deliberated judiciously, "it may be so, and then again it may not."

"I don't see it." Joe felt sharp disappointment at his father's qualified approval. It seemed to him that the return of the safe merited something stronger.

That Mr. Bronson fully comprehended the way Joe felt about it was clearly in evidence, for he went on: "As to the matter of the safe, all hail to you, Joe! Credit, and plenty of it, is your due. Mr. Tate and myself have already spent five hundred dollars in attempting to recover it. So important was it that we have also offered five thousand dollars reward, and but this morning were considering the advisability of increasing the amount. But, my son,"—Mr. Bronson stood up, resting a hand affectionately on his boy's shoulder,— "there are certain things in this world which are of still greater importance than gold, or papers which represent what gold may buy. How about *yourself?* That's the point. Will you sell the best possibilities of your life right now for a million dollars?"

Joe shook his head.

"As I said, that's the point. A human life the money of the world cannot buy; nor can it redeem one which is misspent; nor can it make full and complete and beautiful a life which is dwarfed and warped and ugly. How about yourself? What is to be the effect of all these strange adventures on your life — *your* life, Joe? Are you going to pick yourself up to-morrow and try it over again? or the next day? or the day after? Do you understand? Why, Joe, do you think for one moment that I would place against the best value of my son's life the paltry value of a safe? And *can* I say, until time has told me, whether this trip of yours could not possibly have been better? Such an experience is as potent for evil as for good. One dollar is exactly like another — there are many in the world: but no Joe is like my Joe, nor can there be any others in the world to take his place. Don't you see, Joe? Don't you understand?"

Mr. Bronson's voice broke slightly, and the next instant Joe was sobbing as though his heart would break. He had never understood this father of his before, and he knew now the pain he must have caused him, to say nothing of his mother and sister. But the four stirring days he had lived had given him a clearer view of the world and humanity, and he had always possessed the power of putting his thoughts into speech; so he spoke of these things and the lessons he had learned — the conclusions he had drawn from his conversations with 'Frisco Kid, from his intercourse with French Pete, from the graphic picture he retained of the *Reindeer* and Red Nelson as they wallowed in the trough beneath him. And Mr. Bronson listened and, in turn, understood.

"But what of 'Frisco Kid, father?" Joe asked when he had finished.

"Hum! there seems to be a great deal of promise in the boy, from what you say of him." Mr. Bronson hid the twinkle in his eye this time. "And, I must confess, he seems perfectly capable of shifting for himself."

"Sir?" Joe could not believe his ears.

"Let us see, then. He is at present entitled to the half of five thousand dollars, the other half of which belongs to you. It was you two who preserved the safe from the bottom of the Pacific, and if you only had waited a little longer, Mr. Tate and myself would have increased the reward."

"Oh!" Joe caught a glimmering of the light. "Part of that is easily arranged. I simply refuse to take my half. As to the other — that is n't exactly what 'Frisco Kid desires. He wants friends — and — and — though you did n't say so, they are far higher than money, nor can money buy them. He wants friends and a chance for an education, not twenty-five hundred dollars."

"Don't you think it would be better for him to choose for himself?"

"Ah, no. That's all arranged."

"Arranged?"

"Yes, sir. He's captain on sea, and I'm captain on land. So he's under my charge now."

"Then you have the power of attorney for him in the present negotiations? Good. I'll make you a proposition. The twenty-five hundred dollars shall be held in trust by me, on his demand at any time. We'll settle about yours afterward. Then he shall be put on probation for, say, a year — in our office. You can either coach him in his studies, for I am confident now that you will be up in yours hereafter, or he can attend night-school. And after that, if he comes through his period of probation with flying colors, I'll give him the same opportunities for an education that you possess. It all depends on himself. And now, Mr. Attorney, what have you to say to my offer in the interests of your client?"

"That I close with it at once."

Father and son shook hands.

"And what are you going to do now, Joe?"

"Send a telegram to 'Frisco Kid first, and then hurry home."

"Then wait a minute till I call up San Andreas and tell Mr. Tate the good news, and then I'll go with you."

"Mr. Willis," Mr. Bronson said as they left the outer office, "the San Andreas safe is recovered, and we'll all take a holiday. Kindly tell the clerks that they are free for the rest of the day. And I say," he called back as they entered the elevator, "don't forget the office-boy."

THE
END